Metaphorosis

March 2022

Beautifully made speculative fiction

Also from Metaphorosis

Metaphorosis Magazine

Metaphorosis: Best of 20xx
Metaphorosis 20xx: The Complete Stories
annual issues, from 2016

Monthly issues

Plant Based Press

Best Vegan Science Fiction & Fantasy
annual issues, 2016-2020

from B. Morris Allen:
Chambers of the Heart: speculative stories
Susurrus
Allenthology: Volume I
Tocsin: and other stories
Start with Stones: collected stories
Metaphorosis: a collection of stories

Verdage

Reading 5X5 x2: Duets
Score – an SFF symphony
Reading 5X5: Readers' Edition
Reading 5X5: Writers' Edition

Vestige

The Nocturnals, by Mariah Montoya

Metaphorosis

March 2022

edited by
B. Morris Allen

ISSN: 2573-136X (online)
ISBN: 978-1-64076-224-4 (e-book)
ISBN: 978-1-64076-225-1 (paperback)

Metaphorosis
a magazine of speculative fiction
from
Metaphorosis Publishing

Neskowin

March 2022

Hope on the Vine

R.E. Dukalsky

It was early August and hope was withering on the vine.

It had withered every year so far for the last eleven, so Nima was disappointed rather than surprised. Disappointed, frustrated, demoralized. She really thought she'd gotten the balance right this time.

She knelt in front of the raised mound of earth that should have been nourishing the hope vine's roots, her dirty boots poking out behind her and the sun glinting gently off her greying curls. By this point in the season, the vine should be about three feet tall, with multiple spurs twining eight to ten feet in every direction. Heavy buds the size of the first knuckle of her thumb should be swelling between pairs of reniform leaves gleaming a lustrous dark jade. She should be out here looking eagerly for the first open blossom, a rich yellow stellate flower the size of her hand, shading to the orange of glowing embers in the center. She hadn't seen one for many years.

Instead, she stared disconsolately at a meager vine supporting a few anemic yellow-green spurs. The remaining leaves, with two notable exceptions, were the same undernourished shade, their ribs showing more starkly every day, while their edges turned brown and flaked away. Only one spur, the one that twisted around the rail of the fence, showed any semblance of health, and Nima was as baffled by its continued vitality as she was by the parent vine suddenly giving up on life. It had seemed to be growing on schedule — perhaps a little undersized but a good color — but instead of progressing to the next stage of growth and putting out buds, it had drooped, retreated, withered. Just like its ten predecessors — those that had even bothered to sprout.

Eleven long years on this struggling piece of earth, trying to tease a hope vine from seed to fruit. So far, this was the closest she had come to success. One fruit was all one could expect from such a young vine, but one was all she needed: proof she could send to her Arbiter that this vine would thrive. Then, at last, she could move on. On to the next impoverished, war-scarred town and the next desiccated, abandoned farm, where the potential for hope or fortitude or patience lay dormant under years of neglect and acres of weeds.

The next, and the next, and the next. One by one until the tired land put the years of war and sorrow behind it for good and all.

But there wouldn't be a next and a next if she couldn't bring this vine back to life. Nima doubted she'd live to see the land restored, but leaving here would be its own reward. She dreaded another roasting summer and dreary winter in the small blue house behind her. Another year of being ignored by her neighbors, loathing them in return, and never forgetting no one wanted her here.

Maybe she hadn't fertilized enough? But no; she'd been side-dressing the vine with the recommended half-cup of the special expensive blend that came from the Wizard's Herbarium, and she marked each application on her calendar so she knew she hadn't missed any. Was the mix itself wrong? They said it was guaranteed, but you never knew what that meant with the wizards you got these days. In her time, guarantees had come with blood, not a letter under shiny gilt seal.

If the mix was good, was water the issue? Possible, but hope vines were notoriously flexible in their water needs. In theory, they could take root and grow anywhere, with minimal tending. That was why they, along with fortitude trees and hedges of patience, were among the first recommended plants for war restoration project sites. Even someone who'd never set finger to a garden should be able to grow one — and once a hope vine established itself, every living thing in the area would flourish as well.

Probably she hadn't figured out the right tending regimen. This was where hope vines could be tricky, according to both her own vague memories and the instructions she received each year with the new seed. Fortitude trees could be watered with either sweat or blood (both of which she had in abundance, particularly in the summer). A hedge of patience would grow well with tears, sighs or, in a pinch, prayers. Hope vines demanded fiddly, intangible things: dreams recounted, promises exchanged, plans laid. But wizards didn't dream, she had no one to make promises to, and under the circumstances plans were not hers to lay. She'd tried making promises to the old farmhouse, to the wasted land around it, to the rickety fence and the empty road, but she wasn't sure they counted. If she were honest, the only promise she meant to keep was the one about leaving.

She'd walk out the gate now and never come back if she hadn't given her word, and not with some fancy seal, but in the old way, with consequences for breaking her oath. She'd promised to stay until she could prove she'd restored local resilience to an acceptable baseline — in plainspeak, until the hope vine was able (or willing?) to reproduce. No one back in the capital knew, or really cared, how long it took or what it asked of the grower. The point was to have wizards scattered across the land, repairing the scars of war where everyone could see them doing it.

So here she was until she could cultivate her release.

Nima stroked a finger across one of the limp leaves. "If you stay alive, I leave and you never have to see me again. So save us both some pain and just *grow*," she whispered, putting all the force of her will into it. No effect, of course, except a dull burn up her right arm to complement her aching knees.

"What's wrong with your plant?"

The voice was high-pitched and unfamiliar. Nima looked up to see a girl of about twelve years draped across the fence near the gate ten feet away. Just about where the questing ends of the vine ought to be right now, Nima thought sourly. She'd never seen the girl before, though she had the look of a local: a short, wide body, tawny skin, a blunt nose, and straight, thick black hair cut short above her shoulders. Her eyes were close-set, small, and twinkling with curiosity.

"It isn't growing," Nima said shortly. She was sick to death of these suspicious locals. "Did you need something?"

"I'm Yun," the girl said, completely ignoring the pointed question. "Did you forget to water it?"

"No," Nima replied, trying to rein in her temper. It wouldn't improve her relationship with the locals if she started yelling at children. On the other hand, she didn't care that much about having a relationship with the locals. She turned back to the hope vine, scratching gently in the dirt around the main stalk to see if there was something preying on its roots.

"What about fertilizing? Did you feed it?" Yun asked.

"Yes," Nima said without looking up.

"Did you put it in the right kind of soil?"

"*Yes.*"

"Does it get enough sun?"

Exasperated, Nima gestured at the open sky. Her back twinged, and she looked up with an even more unfriendly expression than she'd intended.

"Hm. Maybe it's getting *too* much sun," Yun mused, unfazed. "Or maybe this isn't a good place for it to grow."

Nima clenched her jaw and bent back down. Maybe the irritating child would get bored and wander away. After a few seconds she heard soft footsteps against the dust and dared to hope. But no luck.

"But I don't know," Yun said, from much nearer, almost right in front of

Nima. "It *feels* like it wants to grow here." A brown hand appeared at the corner of Nima's vision, stroking the leaves of the one remaining spur.

Nima looked up sharply. "Don't touch it," she snapped.

Yun whipped her hand away and looked, for the first time, as if she were picking up on Nima's unwelcoming demeanor. "Why not?"

"Because it's *my* vine," Nima replied, hearing how ridiculous she sounded even as the words came out of her mouth. "What I mean is, it's fragile and it isn't polite to touch other people's crops."

This was evidently a new concept to Yun. "I help Aunt Lio with her beans all the time and she says—"

But Nima was done with this conversation she hadn't wanted in the first place. She didn't want what passed for local agricultural expertise, especially from a child, and needed peace and quiet to think about what to try next. "Then I'm sure she would appreciate your help now," she interrupted, then stood up and stalked away, pushing through the stiffness in her knees. "Don't touch my plants," she called over her shoulder without looking back.

Working on a half-baked theory that her bad mood was somehow hampering the vine's growth, Nima stayed away from it for the next few days. She kept a sharp eye on the fence, but the girl had vanished back to whatever ramshackle farmhouse she'd come from. Nima saw her traipsing by once on the road, but the girl showed no inclination to stop or pester the vine.

After a week, Nima woke up having slept well, and decided she'd waited enough time to test her theory. If her mood did somehow affect the vine, she'd given it time to recover and should be able to see the effects. She filled her big watering can, sprinkled in the special water-soluble fertilizer and lugged it out to the fence.

The vine looked exactly the same: anemic stalk and spurs, withered yellow leaves slowly crumbling off their ribs... and one perfectly healthy spur climbing slowly around the fence rail along the road. The good spur had even put out another two leaves while the rest of the plant died.

"What...?" Nima stood there, hands hanging down open at her sides. She had learned to grow things; the profusely healthy vegetable garden behind the house attested to that. She glared at the vine, disregarding the theory she'd been testing. "What do you *want* from me?" There was no reason this should be so hard, no reason this spur should thrive while the parent plant died, no reason the one plant that mattered should wither while the rest of the garden flourished.

A sharp trill pierced her despair. Yun was tromping down the road in heavy boots several sizes too big for her, swinging two empty beaten metal buckets, whistling like the cloudy morning had been made for her alone. There was something odd about the buckets; they were the wrong shape somehow, too rounded on the bottom, with asymmetric sides. Nima squinted at them and realized they were infantry helmets, inexpertly beaten into a slightly more bucket-like shape by a *very* amateur blacksmith.

"Did you figure out how to fix your plant?" Yun asked. She must have taken Nima's attempt to parse the helmets-turned-buckets as an invitation to stop and chat.

"No," Nima said, trying to think of a task that would take her away from the fence but allow her to keep an eye on the girl.

"It looks better, though," Yun said, waving one of the buckets at the flourishing spur. At least she wasn't trying to touch it. She wrinkled her nose. "That part, at least."

Nima picked up her watering can and began dribbling the water gently around the roots of the vine. Yun didn't take the hint. She tromped a few steps closer, set the buckets down with a dusty *thump*, and squatted on her haunches in front of the vine. "I think it's happier on this side of the fence."

"Plants don't feel happy or sad," Nima said repressively. She saw Yun shrug out of the corner of her eye.

"Aunt Lio says they do." Aunt Lio was evidently the arbiter of reality. She leaned closer. "What kind of plant is this anyway?"

"A hope vine," Nima said shortly, then surprised herself by continuing, "at least, it's supposed to be."

"I never saw one of those before," Yun said, scrunching up her nose and peering at the plant with renewed interest.

"They aren't very common after the war," Nima found herself explaining.

"Ah," Yun said sagely, although she wasn't old enough to remember even the final years of the war and couldn't possibly understand what lay behind the disappearance of the country's native resilient vegetation. "What's it for?"

For giving you and all your ungrateful kin a future worth growing into, Nima thought but did not say. The last thing she wanted was this girl's irate aunt descending to put the wizard in her place. "If it grows," she said, biting off each word, "it will reinforce the local ecosystem — that means the soil, the water, other plants, the animals that eat those plants, and people who rely on the plants and animals," she added, confident that the local school, if one even existed, did not cover the ecology of resilience.

"We have been having some problems," Yun agreed thoughtfully, just as if she were a grizzled veteran farmer. She leaned even closer to the vine, body rolling at such an angle that Nima feared she would pitch face first into the plant — and the railing.

"Be careful," she said, more harshly than she had intended.

Yun straightened up, but didn't look abashed. "I think maybe this part of the plant isn't bothered by something that's messing with the rest of it," she said. "Or maybe it just likes that I talk to it."

Yun's comment niggled at the back of Nima's brain. Maybe there *was* something affecting the roots or the leaves on the parent vine that hadn't spread to the healthy spur yet — or maybe the spur had some kind of natural resistance...

"I have to go restake the beans," Yun was saying in the background, but Nima was no longer paying attention. She didn't even notice the girl stretching out a stealthy hand to give the new leaves a friendly tap. "I'll be back tomorrow."

Yun kept turning up after that. Sometimes for an hour, sometimes for ten minutes, sometimes carrying her ridiculous repurposed buckets, sometimes hauling a feed sack on a little wagon, frequently with her arms full of hollow reeds as wide as her wrist and as tall as she was. She never seemed to be in a hurry or fear that whoever sent her on these tasks would be impatient at her dawdling. Aunt Lio either ran a slipshod operation or didn't particularly care what this niece was up to. Yun never mentioned her parents, so maybe she was a war orphan dumped on her only known relative. Maybe Lio had so much help on her farm that one lolly-gagging child made no difference. Or maybe they were just relieved to get a break from her questions.

"Do they have hope vines where you come from?" she asked one time.

"No," Nima said.

"Then how do you know how to grow one?"

I don't, Nima thought. "Resilient plants need the same things as any other plants —"

"Where *do* you come from anyway?" Yun interrupted.

"Not here," Nima said, picking up her rake and walking away.

"I know this isn't your farm," Yun said another time.

Nima was pruning back the dead leaves on the spurs closest to the healthy one, in case the problem was some kind of spore or mildew. Her shears jumped and nearly clipped a healthy leaf. "What is that supposed to mean?" she demanded.

"Everyone knows you aren't from here, even though you've lived here forever," Yun said with a limber shrug. "When are the people who belong to this farm coming back?"

"They aren't," Nima snapped.

"Maybe this would grow better if they did," Yun said, bumping the vine with grimy knuckles.

"Don't touch," Nima said, but she'd long since given up on the idea that Yun would listen.

"Don't worry, *I'm* not going away," Yun said, more to the vine than to Nima. "Hey look, there's a new grabby bit here!"

"How does a hope vine help the... ecosystem?" Yun asked after she'd been coming by regularly for almost a month.

"Different ways," Nima said distractedly, her words punctuated by the *thonk-crunch* of her trowel. She was digging some small trenches to drain excess water away from the hope vine's mound just in case the roots were becoming waterlogged. "Other things ...

grow better … near a hope vine. Fewer diseases … more abundant production. Roots … stop erosion and make dead soil fertile again. You can live … off a single fruit … for a long time. Healing tea or tincture from the leaves. And just being around the flowers…" she sat back on her heels and wiped her forehead, "I really can't explain what that feels like, you have to experience it for yourself."

"We could really use one of those," Yun said. "Aunt Lio says the beans need a miracle."

"Hope vines aren't miracles, they're applied magic," Nima said sternly. "And you shouldn't expect either to do your work for you."

"I am doing the work," Yun said, but without heat. "But there's a bug that came and it eats the buds before they can bloom." She reached a finger out toward the vine, then pulled it back again.

"What's it like?" Yun asked on one unreasonably hot day.

"What's what like?" Nima replied, only half listening as she teased a tendril gently through a gap in the climbing frame.

"Being a bad wizard."

Nima froze with the tendril balanced on one finger. "What do you mean by that?" she asked carefully. Sweat trickled between her shoulder blades.

"Everyone knows," Yun said without noticeable concern. "You're a bad wizard who made all the bad stuff happen in the war."

Nima snatched her hand away from the vine so she wouldn't transmit her feelings through the tender shoots. "That's a gross exaggeration."

"Also, I saw your thing," Yun pointed at Nima's right arm, where the geas runes constraining Nima's magic and her free movement crawled with slow abandon. She'd probably spotted it the first time they met, but Nima found herself tugging her sleeve down anyway, angry at her own shame. She hated any reminder that she was permanently separated from her magic, even though she'd accepted the geas binding to avoid lifetime imprisonment.

"Aunt Lio says getting a nice farm to run isn't a real punishment," Yun persisted. She reached out and casually flicked the vine. Nima winced, but the vine held firm. In fact, it flexed a tendril toward the sun.

Nima picked up her trowel, hefted it, set it down. She didn't like the idea of Yun and her aunt discussing her sentence as if were just moderately interesting village gossip. "Your Aunt Lio doesn't know everything. It's not a punishment. It's a collective obligation."

"Hah!" Nima wasn't sure whether Yun's hard, fierce laugh was meant to dismiss the possibility that Aunt Lio could be wrong or the official line that felt flat even to the wizard herself. "Then why do you have that?" Yun jabbed a finger at the geas runes.

"Yes, fine, technically it's a punishment," Nima said sharply, "but I *cooperated*. I *agreed* to community service. I could have just done my time, but I entered the program voluntarily to try to make amends for what happened. Nobody forced me to wear this." She shook her right arm at the girl. "Nobody forced me to be here."

"Then why don't you leave?" Yun asked in genuine curiosity.

In all the years she'd endured in this place, no one had ever asked Nima what she thought about her situation. It was humiliating to be grateful for a child's fickle attention, but her life was nothing but humiliations now.

"Because what the wizards did was wrong," Nina said, striving for patience. Not native to this farm and not native to her either. "We had the right — we had good intentions. But we did things that had consequences far beyond what we intended, beyond what we could have imagined when we started."

"What were you trying to do?" Yun asked. "Aunt Lio says all you wizards just wanted to keep your power and when the war happened you decided to burn the country down instead of sharing even one good thing with regular people."

There had been a time where Nima would have drowned in their own sweat anyone who dared speak so harshly, so honestly. "How fortunate that a bean farmer knows the absolute truth!" she snapped, then reined herself in. "Look, the war was complicated and you're too young to understand most of what happened."

Yun crossed her arms, stubborn. "Aunt Lio says the wizards hoarded all the best food and medicine and magic in their towers," she persisted. "She says the headwomen of all the villages went to the towers and asked for the wizards to share, but the wizards said they had nothing valuable to trade. So the villages stopped sending tithes to the towers and then the wizards came out of their towers and ruined everything. And Tonji says the wizards never loved anything but themselves and that's why they could do what they did to the land and the rivers and everything."

Nima had no idea who Tonji was and she didn't like their assessment of the war. "That's not an accurate picture," she said stiffly, although it was, if boiled down to its essence and told through the eyes of the victors. "There was... more to it." In the back of her mind she heard, was always hearing, the soul-shattering crack of her tower's foundations.

"Like what?" Yun asked pugnaciously.

Nima thought of her tower, its dimensions aligned precisely with the planes and angles of her interior self. Like a phantom limb, she could feel vast power seeping from the land into her tower's stones, and from its stones into her. Power that extended the reach of her hand as far as thought could take it, that honed her vision, peering keen-edged with magic into any secret she desired. When her tower stood, she was the secret composer of the song beneath everything... and then they had pulled her tower down and she was nothing. Keeper of a withered garden in a mutilated land. Bitterness welled up in her.

"I couldn't possibly explain it to you in a way you could comprehend," she said, aiming for austere, but coming no higher than cruel.

Yun gave her a very straight look then shrugged deliberately. "Well, it's not like you know the first thing about growing beans," she replied.

It toppled Nima like she was a tower herself. Yun hadn't spoken in pettiness, but rather with the world-weary familiarity of someone who often had to defend her own worth. Maybe she'd heard her aunt use the line and seen the seed of truth it held. Yun didn't know what it was like to wield power that could make and unmake the world. Nima didn't know how to grow beans. Once, the difference between them would have been too vast to comprehend. Now, it meant that between the two of them, Nima was merely the less capable subsistence farmer.

Nima was used to wrapping prickly defensiveness around herself like armor, but she suddenly couldn't reach it. They just sat there looking at each other, black eyes to brown. "I never had any reason to grow beans before," Nima said, conceding.

The silence stretched for several more minutes while Nima pretended to rearrange the dirt at the base of the vine's main stalk. "Wizards cared for the land a long time," she continued at last. "People couldn't see what we did. For generations we kept the soil fertile, managed the weather, sustained the forests...we didn't intend to destroy so much, not when the rebellion started and not after. We were just desperate to make the war stop."

Yun tilted her head skeptically. "If you wanted the war to stop, you could have just given the headwomen what they asked for. You didn't have to do all that bad stuff," she said.

Nima had used a lot of noble sentences and fine words to get her through the dark nights of doubt, but none of them volunteered to stand up against that unflinching logic. "You're right," she said, after a long minute. "But we did do it. I. I did it. All I can do now is try to repair what I can."

Yun glanced away as if the subject had never really been that interesting in the first place. "So why is this vine so important?"

Nima scrubbed her hands over her face. "This land, one of the things it has — had —" she paused. Started again. "A long time ago, wizards found a way to cultivate resilience. *Yes, wizards,*" she snarled at the skeptical look on Yun's face. "They taught seeds to grow hope, patience, and fortitude. They infused rivers with trust and stocked lakes with solidarity. They showed the land how to produce the things that would sustain it, no matter what came." She pressed her lips together and bit down hard on the sour feeling twisting her belly. "But the hope vines and trees of fortitude and all the rest of it didn't survive the war."

"Because of you," Yun interrupted. "You wizards, I mean. Right?"

"It wasn't just—" But it was. They had stretched out their hands and stripped the land of everything their forebears had grafted into it. She was out here trying to make amends for her role in that enormous crime, so what was the point of spinning a sweeter-sounding version of the truth to this child who wasn't buying it anyway? "Yes. Wizards weren't responsible for all the bad things that happened in the war, but they — we — did destroy the resiliency ecosystem. We did that."

"Why?" Yun asked.

A simple, deadly question. Nima had answers she'd given herself, answers she'd given her colleagues who doubted their course of action, answers she'd given the court that sentenced her.

Only we have the knowledge and experience to guide this country to its better future. Our better future requires peace and peace requires order, and order can only come when the villages bow to our authority.

These rebel armies are destroying the land — perhaps if they see harsh consequences they will surrender before we have to kill them all.

Some of the Wizard's Consortium chose to cross that final line and the rest of us let ourselves get pulled across.

So many answers. But none of them sufficient, in the end, to justify stripping the land of everything that held it together and helped it thrive. Not when you boiled it down to a young girl and an old wizard crouched on opposite sides of a fence in a dusty nowhere trying to understand why nothing good could grow.

"Because we forgot that wizards first built towers to serve and protect the land," she said at last. She suddenly became aware of how stiff and heavy her legs had become. "We thought of the land as something under our rule, not under our care. So when the rebels — when the war came, it was easy to use the land as a weapon."

Nima remembered standing atop her tower filled with grim righteousness as she stretched out her hands and drained the Ko River into the bedrock. She remembered the sense of urgency that filled her heart when she walked in the fortitude groves, blighting the ancient trees to strip the rebels of their will to fight. She remembered having those feelings, but she couldn't reproduce them. Now, all she could feel was shame and despair at the enormity of what they had done. How could she ever have thought that growing one stupid hope vine would mean anything in the face of their atrocities? Even if she lived to be the oldest wizard in history and grew a new vine or tree every year, it would be a pitiful drop in the desert their crimes had created.

"And now wizards must undo what wizards did," Yun chanted the first line of the decree that doomed all surviving wizards to a lifetime of penal restitution — out here in the backlands, it was probably the only part of the decree she'd ever heard. She bopped one of the withered leaves unceremoniously. "You're not very good at it, huh?"

Nima lurched forward to cup the leaf, jerked herself back, then stared at it as it seemed to stretch out luxuriously. Was a deeper green flushing outward from the central rib, or were her eyes lying to her? "This work is much harder than I expected," she admitted.

Yun nodded sagely. "I bet it's hard to make this place hopeful when you aren't." Then her head shot up as if hearing a voice calling her. "Whoops, gotta go," she said. She hopped to her feet, scooped up her buckets, and took off at a steady trot down the road.

Nima watched her go, rolling her last words around and around. *It's hard to make this place hopeful when you aren't.* That could be the problem. Perhaps the hope vine couldn't grow if its tender had no hope of her own to share.

But then — Nima leaned over the leaf Yun had bopped, without touching it herself. It was noticeably greener and drooped less. And then — she peered down where Yun had been flicking her careless fingers, and there was one, no two! new tendrils peeking out. Nima thought about all the times she'd scolded Yun for touching the vine. Was it a coincidence that the healthy spur was the one closest to the road, the easiest one for Yun to reach? Was the vine nourishing itself off her innate hope for the future, a future Yun expected to be part of in exactly the way Nima didn't?

Nima brooded on it all night.

Yun came back the next day, and the next, chattering about the problem with Aunt Lio's bean crop. Nima made noncommittal noises or gave answers she forgot even as they came out of her mouth. The beans weren't her problem. She was watching Yun and the vine, trying to learn the secret of how she made it grow.

The girl didn't appear to be doing anything special. She didn't even seem to be paying attention to the vine most of the time, although she always crouched by it when she stopped, even though it meant she had to perch in the ditch on the side of the road. She would bump or stroke or tap the leaves or tendrils to emphasize a point or sometimes as if it were agreeing with her, but she might have done the same thing with her buckets or the wagon. She certainly didn't treat the vine with the care or deference that Nima herself did. Nima couldn't see any one thing that set Yun's interactions with the hope vine above her own — except, of course, that the vine grew where Yun touched it and withered everywhere she did not.

And 'grow' was a bit of an understatement. On Nima's side of the fence, the other spurs had desiccated into dry, spindly stalks, their leaves long since crumbled into the dirt. On Yun's side, seven feet of rich jade green sprouted leaves the size of Nima's palm, twisted tendrils around every surface of the climbing frame and the fence rails, and were sending out new spurs in two places.

There was even one tiny green nub that, given time, would become a bud.

Nima never, ever touched the healthy spur. She even stood on the dead side of the plant to water and dress it, hoping not to poison it with indirect contact. She didn't encourage Yun to touch it either, superstitiously worried that the vine would pick up on her desperation and stop responding to Yun's presence. She just held herself in nervous stasis, waiting for the bloom.

Maybe it was the empty rattling of the sledge that drew Nima's attention, or maybe it was how Yun's feet dragged in the dusty road as she approached. Whatever it was, Nima looked up one day to see a new expression on Yun's face: despair.

The girl squatted in her usual place on the other side of the fence, her hands flopped over her knees and her black hair sticking to her sweaty temples. She didn't touch the vine.

"What's wrong with you?" Nima said, more harshly than she'd intended. But then, she'd never been a gentle person.

"The bean crop failed," Yun said, looking burdened in a way Nima had never seen her. "Aunt Lio says there's no way to save it now, even though we built reed irrigation all the way from the river and I pick off all the bugs I can find."

"I guess you'll have to eat something other than beans this winter," Nima said, trying to remember if beans had some sort of local cultural significance. "Variety is good for you."

Yun looked at her like Nima had just suggested they try to eat the sun. "We don't eat beans, we sell them," she said. Then, in a cadence that sounded like something she'd heard from someone else many times, "No beans, no money. No money, no winter stores, no shoes, no seeds for spring."

"Oh," Nima said. Of course Yun's entire livelihood hung on those stupid beans. "That's...bad."

Yun sighed heavily and gave the swollen bud close to her face the gentlest of caresses. Nima sucked in her breath, but Yun didn't notice and the vine didn't show any immediate negative effects. "Do you know any way to fix the beans?" she asked suddenly, looking a little nervous for the first time Nima could remember. "I mean…I know you said we shouldn't expect magic to fix our problems, but you also said wizards used to take care of the land…"

"Not with this," Nima said, jerking her right arm in a sharp motion so the geas runes caught the light.

"Oh, right," Yun said, subsiding back despondently. She sighed again. "We sure could use one of these hope vines right now." Nima suddenly recognized the line as something she'd heard Yun saying a lot lately.

That night, Nima found herself thinking of Yun's beans instead of the hope vine. There wasn't any reason to be thinking about either one — all she could do for the vine was what she'd done, and Yun was someone else's problem — but she kept coming back to it like a piece of food stuck between her molars. It wasn't just the girl's despair; Nima hadn't spent a century as a powerful wizard with a tower of her own because she was susceptible to sad peasant children. But what if the bean crop's failure forced Yun and her family to leave the farm? What if they starved? What would happen to the hope vine if Yun suddenly stopped coming by, telling her cheerful stories and helping pass the long weary days with impertinent questions?

And more than that — Yun's intervention, however unintentional, had resuscitated Nima's own hope of escaping this pastoral prison. Which, in a way, put her in Yun's debt.

And that was the nub of the problem, Nima realized as she dried her dinner dishes. She felt indebted to Yun, who had helped her while enduring Nima's constant unwelcoming attitude. And there was a way to repay her. But it would cost Nima the one thing she valued: the opportunity to leave.

On the other hand, if she didn't pay this debt, Nima would be proving Aunt Lio and Tonji right: that wizards would rather let the land and everyone who depended on it suffer than share even one good thing. And even more than she hated being in debt, more than she hated being here, Nima found she hated the idea that Lio and her ilk could be right about her after all. If they were, then Yun would keep believing they were right about the war, would keep thinking wizards were bad people who embraced destruction to feed their own selfishness.

"Damn and damn!" she swore, looking down to discover she'd worried her washing cloth into threads.

She couldn't repair the land. She couldn't undo the systemic destruction they'd wrought, not even in a wizard's lifetime.

She could save one bean farm. She could persuade one girl — maybe one family — that wizards could help as well as harm. Not just for show, or to win release, but because she wanted Yun to welcome a future with wizards in it as enthusiastically as she welcomed everything else. It would cost at least a year of her life; there was no guarantee that this hope vine would fruit two years in a row. But after eleven years of loneliness and failure, was one more really such a sacrifice?

"Yes it *is*," Nima snarled to the empty room, to herself. "But wizards must undo what wizards did." Then she picked up her lamp and stomped out of the house.

Hope vines thrived on promises, after all.

Nima waited with characteristic impatience for Yun to arrive the next morning, but the girl didn't appear until mid-afternoon, trudging along in her too-big boots and carrying her mangled helmet buckets. She flashed Nima a wan smile as she crouched down by the vine, petting it as if seeking comfort from the silky leaves.

"How are the beans?" Nima asked awkwardly after a minute. She hadn't thought about this part, not once she'd made her decision. And, she realized, she'd never started one of their conversations before today. It was always Yun, interrupting her work with a question or observation.

"Still bad," Yun said. "Aunt Lio says we'll be lucky to get a quarter of the crop."

"Well, look," Nima said, her eyes fixed on the hope vine while her hands fiddled anxiously in the dirt. "This thing is about to flower. If it fruits, I could — you could have it. You could plant it near your beans. I'm sure it would grow for you."

Yun looked up, her eyes shining in a way Nima had never seen. It was like all the dust had washed right out of her world. "You mean it? We could have a hope vine of our own?"

"It won't make your bean plants come back," Nima warned. "Probably."

"But it means they'll grow good next year!" Yun said with an enormous grin. "That's right, isn't it? Everything grows better where a hope vine grows?"

"That's the theory," Nima agreed. She felt surprisingly guilty giving the girl hope when she wasn't sure the vine was capable of producing a fruit this late in the season. But then, hope was all she had to offer, from beginning to end.

"But... wait." Yun crinkled up her face around her nose. "Don't you have to send that fruit to your Arbiter? So they send you on to your next place?"

"There will be another fruit, in another year," Nima said with forced calm, giving the vine an affectionate little stroke with the back of her hand. And to her utter astonishment, a tiny bright green tendril unfurled from beneath her knuckles.

The vine bloomed four days later, opening like a star and drawing the eye from anywhere in the garden. Nima found herself staring at it for uncounted time, just tracing its silky depths with her eyes.

She could see, if she looked closely in the way wizards were trained to do, runes tracing and retracing themselves deep within the flower's genetic structure. But mostly she just stood beside the vine, falling into its radiance.

Two days after the bloom, Nima came out early to gaze at the flower. It was a habit she'd fallen into immediately, getting in close to the luminous petals, tracing the dew that beaded gently on their surface, filling her lungs with the flower's scent before facing the tasks of the day. It made the whole day seem more bearable; no, it made tomorrow seem so promising it was worth today's labor.

At the cottage door she gasped in horror; even from that distance she could see the blossom was withered, almost completely gone after only two days. What would she tell Yun? How had she killed the flower so quickly even when everything seemed to be going well?

But when she drew close, crouching down and parting the leaves with trembling hands, she saw the flower had died a purely natural death. Hope blossomed fleetingly, it seemed, or perhaps her decision had hurried it along. There, glowing greeny-golden as a brand-new promise, a small orb poked up from the heart of the crumpled petals.

The vine's first fruit.

See R.E. Dukalsky's story "Hope on the Vine" online at Metaphorosis.
If you liked it, leave a comment. Authors love that!
Remember to subscribe to our e-mail updates so you'll know when new stories are posted.

About the story

"Hope on the Vine" grew from two very different seeds. In my non-writing professional life, I work on peace processes, political transitions, and rule of law, which means I spend a lot of time thinking about the aftermath of conflict. In my reading experience, speculative fiction tends to focus on how conflicts begin, how they are fought, or how they end — but not the long generational slog toward (or away from) peace that comes after. (In this, spec fic mirrors "real" life in countries that observe, but haven't recently experienced, conflict.) It's not just about rebuilding shattered infrastructure; it's also about restoring trust between communities, keeping peace talk promises, and demonstrating the will to make a future different from the past. Making peace also requires that societies acknowledge the wrongs committed in the past, hold the perpetrators accountable, and try to repair what can be repaired (a series of processes collectively called transitional justice). It's hard, slow work with many steps sideways or backward as well as forward, requiring change in systems and institutions but also in individual hearts.

One of the most difficult elements to rebuild after conflict are the characteristics that help societies hold together.   These intangibles are often vaguely categorized as "resiliency factors," and they include trust, tolerance, a sense of a shared future, community solidarity, and, yes, hope. This story is an attempt to envision what transitional justice might look like in a world with magic, where resiliency factors are tangible things. I wanted to write about a perpetrator coming to terms with both her own past crimes and her role in repairing the greater harm to which those crimes contributed. I also wanted to look at a world where wizards were held accountable for their deeds, not by a group of brave heroes, but by a court and a system of law. And finally, I wanted to imagine a post-conflict scenario where subsistence farmers finally got some justice.

The other seed for this story is much more literal. I'm terrible at growing squash. I can grow many tasty things and squash are notoriously easy plants, but for some reason they elude me. I've spent many days just like Nima, screaming "why won't you just grow?" at a withering squash vine. Fortunately, my life and freedom have never depended on a zucchini or a kabocha, but I wanted to convey the sense of helpless frustration that comes from doing everything you can think of for a growing thing and still seeing it fail.

So that's where "Hope on the Vine" comes from: meditations on transitional justice and my own gardening mishaps. Hopefully you enjoyed the hybrid they created.

A question for the author

Q: What's your favorite *non*-SFF book?

A: I have never been able to answer this kind of question with just one favorite book. I love *The Secret History of the Mongol Queens* by Jack Weatherford and *King Leopold's Ghost* by Adam Hochschild because they changed the lens through which I saw the world, making it feel bigger and more connected at the same time. Hilary Mantel's *Wolf Hall* will always be among my top books for her complex portrayal of flawed but extremely human characters. *Midnight's Children* by Salman Rushdie got its feverish hooks into my brain over a decade ago and never let go. Ask me this question again in a year and the list might be different, but it won't be any shorter.

About the author

R.E. Dukalsky writes speculative fiction about conflict and what happens afterward. She has been told that she has School House Rock charm and that she would make an excellent rebel leader, among other dubious accolades. She lives in the Pacific Northwest in a house that perpetually needs more bookshelves.

@tiltingwindward

Mission and Submission

Will Gwaun

Amir and Sahia lay side by side in the narrow berth, waiting to hear if there was a home waiting for them out there in the darkness of space. They held hands. In the rhythm of her breath, he felt the pendulum of her thoughts swinging from fear back to hope, and his own thoughts turned to follow.

Years ago, centuries now, Amir had felt in those moments as if he could sense the whole ship holding its breath. He'd once imagined the thousands of crew in the cabins adjoining theirs, some freshly woken from hibernation, some born on board and awake their whole lives, but all in some sense beside him, clinging to that same hope: a planet where, at last, the ship could land. Now, Amir thought of most of those crew as strangers, jealous of his and Sahia's places in hibernation pods. He pressed his body closer to hers, this sliver of warmth and hope in all the vast expanse of nothing and cold. Now, in these moments, he felt nothing beside him but Sahia.

A hologram schematic of the ship's journey so far floated in their optics. Earth, now many trillions of kilometres behind them, winked in the corner of the cabin. From it ran the line of the ship's trajectory, and branching from that, the routes of the probes the ship had launched along the way. Each branch ended at a planet that had promised to be a home; the long-range scans had shown them to be similar enough to Earth. The ship had been turned and steered towards them, launching the close-scanning probes and driving them ahead with powerful lasers. But each time the transmissions from those probes returned, they carried news of disappointment.

Amir ran his finger along that undulating path, remembering the awful dangers each of those planets had concealed. Radiation, tectonic chaos, wild storms hidden by the cloud layer. And never a hint of life.

The ship only carried enough fuel to decelerate once from its astonishing velocity, and none of those planets had been safe enough to justify it. So on they went, changing course after each disappointment and climbing back into the hibernation pods for another long, cold sleep of centuries. At least, that was how it had been. After those first few disappointments, after the hibernation had proven itself less safe than the research had claimed, more and more of the crew had decided to give up on the voyage and live out their lives awake on board the ship.

It should never have been that way. The pods should have preserved their bodies without risk or side effect. But then, no one had thought they'd have to use them so long and so many times. No one had believed that the hope of all those worlds could be false, so no one had thought too deeply about the many and unique ways each individual body might degrade under the strain of dozens of sleep-wake cycles, immune cells turning mutinous, memories fogging in neural debris, chromosomes warping until their cells grew cancerous.

This world ahead of them now, though... This one looked more promising than any yet. They'd learnt from all those disappointments, learnt from the discrepancies between the long-range scans and the close-ups sent from the probes, learnt to filter the signal from the noise masquerading as hints of vital elements and gases, taught their algorithms to pick through the magnetic fields for the toxic thrum of dying atoms. These scans were pure, and this world promised to be the one.

In the hologram, a blip showing the position of the data packet returning from the probes approached the ship with agonising slowness. They should have woken in time with its arrival, but the probes' journey had been delayed by some few hours. It felt like days.

"I dreamt about the world ahead, I think," Sahia murmured in that low voice she used when speaking to herself.

"Yes? What did you see?" Amir asked, amused, as ever, by her surprise that she'd spoken her thoughts aloud.

She rolled onto her side to face him, that teasing glint creeping into her smile. "Other people's dreams are fundamentally impossible to find interesting," she said, quoting a faux pas of his from some fundraising-for-the-mission dinner, a lifetime ago but still funny to them. The teasing sparked a prickle of desire in his stomach, and he slide his hand over her palm, lacing his fingers between hers.

"Not your dreams, Sih, *other people's* dreams." He pouted, impersonating that outrageously-over-rouged heiress-and-possible donor he'd offended at the dinner, quoting the rebuke she'd given: " 'This dream, I assure you, is quite fascinating.' "

He held the raised eyebrow a moment and then dropped the act, lowering his head on the pillow, reaching out to slide her hair back from her cheek. "Please, Sih. I love to hear your dreams." It was true. It felt like a gift to be let into that strange and private world.

They looked at each other for a moment, and the smile she gave him made his heart shiver.

"I don't know." she said. "It's mostly a blur. I was waking from the deep."

The mention of deep sleep made Amir suddenly conscious of the ache in his back and the numbness in his feet. They'd been in deep almost two hundred years. It shouldn't have mattered how long you were down for; it was the waking from deep that took its toll, the draining of the desiccating and freezing agents. He shifted in the bed. At least the ringing in his ears and the thudding in his head had passed.

"You remember something?" he asked.

"In the dream, the sky was lilac, like you said. I want to retract my bet." They always made a bet. On Earth they had both worked on the sensors that performed the scans, and that question about the colour of the sky seemed to be asked at every press or outreach event. One could answer with educated guesses based on refraction and reflection, the fingerprints of gases and starlight. But atmospheres had many layers, so one never knew the sky's colour for certain until the probes punched the clouds, turned their eyes skyward and returned their scans.

"No, no, no." He squeezed her hand. "You bet orange, and we shook."

"Which do you want it to be, though? When we get there and look up at the sky, which do you want to see?"

Blue was the obvious. Blue would likely be the colour of an atmosphere close to Earth's. That might make things easier. But Amir hadn't come all this way to find another Earth. He'd been dreaming of other worlds since he first saw the night sky from somewhere beyond the smog and streetlight haze of the city, young enough to sit on his mother's shoulders and be told how every star was a distant sun where planets might turn, on which life might dwell. Through school and college and post-doc and professorship, he'd done and thought of almost nothing else but ways to look deeper into the dark of space for the tell-tale signals of distant worlds.

"How did it feel in your dream? Being under a sky that colour?" He imagined it, how the settlement would look as it unfolded from the ship, the plans they'd spent decades on coming to fruition in the glow of a lilac noon.

"I could live happily under lilac."

They held hands and watched the blip crawl those last centimetres to the ship.

Amir and Sahia lay side by side on the bed, staring up at the hologram of another useless world.

"I really thought this one was..." she began, but trailed off, the disappointment too heavy, too mundane and miserable to put into words.

There was no avoiding these cycles of hope and disappointment. They could not simply remain in hibernation until a suitable planet was finally found. The length of that slumber had to be decided in advance, and could be neither shortened nor extended. The dosage of freezing and desiccating agents seeded in the tissues had to be measured exactly, and, once there, could not be cleared from the tissues without their destruction.

For those of the crew who wished to avoid using up their lifespan aboard the ship, the routine was to go into hibernation until the moment the probes' scans were due to arrive. They would wake to see the results, hoping to need return only once more into the deepness for the final leg of the journey to the planet they'd call home. Instead, each time they'd woken to learn the planet they'd found had proved to be a failure, like all those before, and they would have to return to hibernation as the ship took them onwards into the darkness.

"It isn't certain it's a failure," Amir said. "Not absolutely, not yet."

But it was. The comms channels flickered with the discussion between a score of different expert groups, each with their own analyses of this world's hidden treachery. There would be a vote soon, but the preliminary polling was so clear that it was hardly worth it. They would go on to the next planet, or at least to the point where the transmissions from the probes would intersect the ship's vector. Three hundred something years of ship time.

On the channels, people were already talking about whether they would take that sleep. Of the thousands of crew, there were still some five hundred like Amir and Sahia, born on Earth and in it for the long haul. The others had peeled off slowly; after six or seven or ten disappointments, they'd decided they couldn't risk the hibernations anymore. They wanted to take a chance at some kind of life on board. The ship held facilities meant to provide the building blocks of the settlement: hydroponic greenhouses and algae vats to feed and clothe them, observatories and laboratories where they might study these uncharted worlds, even spaces for schooling and sports could be made within the inner centrifuge. It was enough to make a life in, so people said.

Amir avoided hearing about the life built by those who'd given up on the journey. Meagre as it must be, there was a siren call feel to it. It could hardly be worse than the cupboard of an apartment he'd grown up in, in that bleak, fume-choked city crumbling into the ocean.

Sahia rolled on her side and stared out of porthole at the stars and the darkness between. "Do you ever think..." she said, and a long silence followed.

He looked at her, the dark rings of her hair coiled on the pillow, the contour of the muscles in her shoulder. Even more beautiful now than in all the years he'd known her.

"What?" he asked.

He heard in her breath the weighing of whether she should finish that thought aloud or not. "You ever think we should have stayed on Earth?" she said at last.

"No," he answered automatically. He hadn't, and even the question provoked a wave of anger he couldn't quite understand. "What is there on Earth?"

"Well, it's not a question of what is, not anymore. But don't you think about the things there were, the things we left behind?"

"Of course I do. But..." he laid his hand on her shoulder. He wanted her to look at him. They were the same age, but his skin looked aged beside hers, ashen and cracked around the knuckles. He tried to remember if he'd noticed that before, but didn't think he had. "The risk is worth it. There're still thousands more stars. There's a world for us out there."

"I don't know. This deep was hard. I mean, the doctors didn't say anything, but it felt harder. Didn't it to you?"

"No." He felt the mood between them slipping, like a wandering comet dragged into the gravity well of some dead star. "Why don't we look at the scans for the next planet? The data from the probe might show us something about them—"

"Not now. I can't just sit here anymore. I want to go walk around a bit, see the habitats." She got up, and he watched her dress. It frightened him. They didn't walk around; the only place to do that was the inner centrifuge, which housed the communal habitats used by the ship-born —the descendants of those crew who'd centuries ago abandoned the hibernation pods and made their lives on board. The long-haulers, those who'd come from Earth and still clung to the plan of sleeping through that long journey, didn't want to know about the lives of those ship-born. That, at least, was the mostly unspoken consensus that Amir felt. Long-haulers didn't really regard ship-born as part of the exodus at all, but rather some detail encountered between Earth's cradle and humankind's destiny in the depths of space. What was the sense in getting to know people, only to go back into a deepness you would not wake from before they and their children and grandchildren were long dead? Long-haulers didn't go up into the inner centrifuge at all. They went from hibernation pod to cabin and back, hoarding all the life they had left for the future, when at last it arrived.

Sahia sat at the end of the bed. Amir lay on his side, staring at a hologram schematic of sensor calibrations for the probes being readied for send-off, not to the next planet they would reach, but to those further ahead, just in case. This was his speciality, the role that had bought him this place on the ship. But in truth he could hardly follow the schematic. The crew who'd given up on the hibernation, and their children and grand- and great-grandchildren, had been refining these technologies for centuries, while Amir lay in hibernation. But whatever advances the ship-born made, he assured himself he could catch up once they finally arrived at the planet. After all, most of what he knew was self-taught. But then, that was back on Earth, with the minds of millions always at his fingertips. The ship rumbled, the drives firing to turn its course by fractions of a degree.

"You should at least go and see what they've built, Amir. It's quite amazing. That whole centrifuge, it's like a jungle, like a village in the jungle. All the metal, everything is hidden. I mean, they've had a long time to do it, but it's still astonishing. Rivers, gardens, even the light through the branches looks enough like the sun."

Amir said nothing. His parents had grown up in a farming village at the edge of the jungle, and spoke of the place with nothing but contempt. A quiet tide of anger was building inside him. Her leaving the lower decks felt like an act of betrayal. "I'm not interested in seeing simulations of a planet we left behind. The course is set; we should be getting ready to go into deep."

She didn't answer for a long time, and when she did, he realised he'd known for a long time what was coming. "I don't know if I can keep doing this, Amir. My bones hurt."

"The medicals say we're both fine." Not everyone had had their luck. Each time they woke, someone they knew had suffered something, and now they heard someone had not woken up at all.

"But how long? How many more times are we going to roll the dice? It was supposed to be the first one we reached. But if there's none? What if there's nowhere else for us?"

"How could there be nowhere?" He'd spent his academic career arguing the opposite. Arguing that advances in scanner technology made it obvious that it was no longer a question of *if* there was a planet somewhere that could support human life, but *which* of the many they should go to first. That the ship was yet to encounter one was just bad luck against good odds. Sahia knew that too. Her career had matched his, always aiming them towards this role, this mission, as if the trajectory of the ship had begun not on the launch pad, but back in the classroom of their elementary school. Somewhere, accelerating along that path, he'd realised he'd fallen in love with her, the only person he'd ever met with dreams as big as his.

"And what if there's somewhere, but we wake up to find we're dying? We could live on board. We're still young enough."

He swiped the hologram away and stared out at the stars beyond the window. "Young enough for what?"

She answered so quietly he barely heard her, but he knew what she was saying. "A life. A life outside of this. All we ever did on Earth was work."

She looked at him, and a part of him he didn't want to listen to felt the sudden urge to agree with her. Study and learn and work, that had been their lives. Through childhood and on, it was their companionship that had made it possible, made the crushing expectations of their parents manageable. Sometimes it was only the solidarity of ten-year-olds that had kept the shame of a less-than-perfect exam result from being too much to bear. He looked back at her, and felt a softening creep in, an opening in his heart.

"Maybe this is more like the home we've been looking for than anything we'd found out there," she said, and the opening slammed suddenly shut.

Was all that work to have been for nothing? Were they people who gave up?

He stood, paced across the room. "What could there be here? This is purgatory. This is prison!"

"Friends. Time for ourselves. I don't know. Time for… There's still work here, you know? Still research being done. People are still part of this project, of going to another world, even if it's not them that reach it, but their children, or their grandchildren."

The word 'children' froze him in place. A word they'd drifted by several times in their lives, though it had never drawn them into its orbit. Even if she wasn't saying it directly, he knew what she was asking. And children meant giving up one's place in the limited number of hibernation pods. That was the protocol that a dozen generations had agreed to on board, while Amir and Sahia and the other long haulers slept. The population had grown. More people wanted a chance in those pods than there were places. So that was the rule. Once you had children, your place was given up, allocated to your children, or if they declined it, by lottery to other hopefuls of their generation.

Amir had been furious when he'd first discovered that such a change in the rules had been made in the absence of those still sleeping. It undermined the very principle of consensus democracy and protection of minorities that should govern the ship and colony-to-be, principles thrashed out in hundreds of hours of pre-launch meetings. But he understood it well enough. Deep in the human mind there was the imperative that the code inside one's genes would have a chance to live forever, one way or another. And besides, he'd seen in the records that there were movements among the ship-born population not to support the hibernation pods at all, that their drain on resources was unnecessary. Terrifying to think what such movements could do if they grew large enough, now that consensus had given way to the wishes of the majority. There were more ship-born than long-haulers now, and more importantly, they were awake while

Amir and the others slept. What could be done to stop them? What good were those principles they'd defined, without some authority to enforce them? Better then, that the ship-born have a stake in the pods' ongoing functioning.

That thought unfroze him, bringing his anger to a boiling rage — that 'they' would have the temerity to make decisions for those like Amir who'd created this entire undertaking in the face of every doubt and opposition.

"So that's what you're telling me? That you're glad we've found nothing? No planet, no home, no risk, no more work." The words blurted from Amir's mouth like gas from a blown airlock. "Now we get to stay on board, where it's nice and safe and nothing changes, and live in tree houses and play happy families? That's what you want, after everything we've given to get here?"

Sahia didn't cry. A hard few years of childhood in the flood camps had crushed that out of her. But there was something that happened to her body, her voice, an inward sagging like a balloon seeping air —the way she'd looked for almost a year when her mother, her only family, had died without warning. "I want some life with you, Amir, that's what I want. Don't you?"

"You think I want to have a family here? This is a society of people who've given up. You think that's the father I want to be?"

Sahia's expression became one of wounded disbelief, one that for a moment he could not fathom, until, by that strange telepathy of long companionship, he realised he knew what she thought he was referring to. Remembered a baking-hot night when they were sixteen, standing on the rooftop of their apartment building. She told him then about another night, a decade before, where she and her mother and father had fought through the flood waters, Sahia and her mother floating on a broken door, her father in the water trying desperately to kick against the current and push them to dry land, hour after hour. She'd told him how, when at last a rescue boat appeared and caught them in its spotlight, she'd watched her father just let go of the door and slide under the water, too exhausted to go on.

She'd said she didn't know how to stop being angry at him for giving up, and he'd felt utterly lost for something helpful to say, felt how profoundly childlike he seemed beside her. That feeling was still there, knotted up among all those other threads that wove together into their marriage. And suddenly that angered him, made him feel as if it were some trick to persuade him to acquiesce to the superiority of her argument, the maturity of her perspective.

"You think I'm talking about *that*?" He was shouting. "You think I'd say a thing like that to persuade you? How low do you think—"

"I'm asking you to have the courage to see what's really in front of us, Ami. Sometimes we have to be brave and just accept change, and what we can't change."

He didn't know what to do with his anger. The weight of what she was asking of him crushed the breath from him, as if a black hole had opened in his future. He left without a word. Marched down the corridor, head down. The ache of the deep still groaned in his joints, but he couldn't stop. If he stayed, he would do what she wanted. He knew that. He couldn't look at her like that and not feel every fibre of his thoughts realign to find a way to offer her solace. And he wouldn't be held to ransom that way. It wasn't fair. So he didn't stop until he reached the inner ring where the pods lay, most already filled with the sleepers who'd returned directly after the disappointment of the scans.

The hibernation process was automated. He only needed to strip off his clothes, lie down in the pod, strap the bands around his arms and thighs, and give the commands. He worked as automatically as the machines, giving the command to put him under for another three hundred years, ready to wake when the next transmissions arrived. The clearance chit flickered on the display. He felt the needles ease into his skin, and the cold begin to spread into his muscles.

It was only as his heart began to slow that he realised what a risk he'd taken, how unfair and stupid his assumption was that she would find out what he'd done and follow him. She would be, should be, angry at him. Furious. There'd been no agreement between them. He'd felt trapped and acted out of anger. He knew she would understand that. But that didn't mean... What if she stayed? What if he woke and she was long dead? The world shrank towards darkness. There was nothing to be done.

Amir lay in his pod waiting for control to return to his muscles. A hologram flickered into life in front of his face, offering him a status update. A cursor blinked, led by the movement of his eyes. Through the glass of the pod's front panel, he could hear the muffled sound of cheers, people calling back and forth through the vast space of the hibernation hall.

With only the movement of his eyes, it was agonisingly slow to pull up Sahia's status. When at last he managed, it glowed orange, showing she was in hibernation, but before he could read more, a message from her overlaid itself across the screen. Sahia's face, smiling that indestructible smile of hers that she wore as armour against all the hardship that life was built from. She looked exhausted, aged, shrunken against her bones, black smears under her eyes. When she spoke, there was the edge of a tremble in her voice.

"Amir, I want you to hear this from me. I've tried many times to record this so you will understand me, but somehow I can't find the words I need, so I will just tell you as clearly as I can. I'm recording this message forty-two years since we last spoke, long in the past for you now. I have been awake for two years now. After you went off... after we argued, I didn't know if I would follow you. I know you were angry at me, and when you went into the deepness without me, I was angry also. But I came with you. I could not leave that argument as our last moment together. But... but there was some mistake. The dosage of hibernating agents was not metabolised correctly, and I woke after forty years. I was very ill, for a long time, and I couldn't help feeling like... like it was your fault. I hated feeling like that, but I couldn't..." She looked away from the camera, her smile wavering, looked back, trying to draw the smile back together, then left its ruins where they lay. "I lived with the shipborn for these last years. I needed it. My hope has returned. I don't think you could hear what I was trying to tell you about how much of me had given up. But living with them here, I feel like, even if the planet is never found, something very special has been created here, and I think you would see the same, if you let yourself come and experience it.

But... I miss you too much, Ami. I miss you, and I hate that you won't ever give this up, but that is what I love you for too. You never give up. I wish I could make this choice with you, but you're in there, and I'm here, so this is all I can offer. You know the next planets that we send probes to. The next four are only just 'maybes', and five is hardly even a 'maybe'. But six is a likely candidate, good as any. My body will most likely not cope with more than four or five more wakings at the very most, so I'm choosing to go into the deepness for the long haul. Till the sixth planet. In my heart... I know it will hurt you to hear this, but in truth I've lost the belief that any of them will be safe for us, even the sixth. But I know there's a chance, and I want to give you as many chances as I can. I want use what chances I have left as intelligently as possible. When I wake for the scans from the sixth, and it's good, I'll still have the strength to go into hibernation for the journey there. With luck I'll have the strength to wake and begin our new life. But if it's another disappointment, I won't go down again. I want to have some life here, and I hope... If we still have no luck, I hope you will want that too. I know that in many ways, this is a gamble, but isn't everything? If things go as I hope they will, I'll see you in two thousand six hundred and twenty-nine years. I love you, Ami."

When the message finished, he lay in the pod, fear and guilt and love and shame all twisting together in his gut. Other messages began to ping on his screen, short blasts of triumphant, congratulatory text from colleagues who'd been with them all the way from earth. 'We did it!' 'Told you it was this one!' 'Last one on the surface buys the drinks!' A realisation formed. The cheering—the scans were back; they'd found a home.

Amir lay beside Sahia, though separated from her by the walls of his pod and hers. He'd looked over the data the probes had returned. The world would be hard, but good enough. Everything he'd dreamed of. The sky in the habitable zone was a warm, reddish brown. He could live under that.

The pod's voice asked him to confirm the length of the hibernation. He closed his eyes, imagining the way it would be as the ship landed and settlement began, as those plans he'd spent his lifetime making finally began to unfold. He imagined his footprint in the dust of that alien world, a moment he'd imagined since childhood, an image he'd drawn over and over with crayon and biro and smart pen in the margins of exercise books, lecture notes and the minutes of departmental meetings. The thought of it pulled on him, a gravity too massive to escape.

The pod urged him to answer. "Please confirm."

The words stuck in his throat. The new world was right there, subjectively only moments away. One quick sleep, and the purpose of these years of struggle would finally be reached. He felt the piled weight of his long-dead family's expectations. They had wanted him to do something sensible, something respectable and safe, medicine, law, had given their lives for him to do that. Only Sahia had kept him from giving into them. Now he was just a button push away from proving he'd been right.

"Please confirm," the pod repeated.

He'd paced their cabin for hours, struggling with the decision, his thoughts tearing against each other in straining equilibrium—a blazing star, neither quite blasting apart nor collapsing, the explosive force of its fusing atoms grasped in the vastness of its own gravity. The guilt of forcing her into a sleep that had almost killed her. His distrust and anger at the ship-born, and yet the hope that their achievements brought him for the future on this at-last-found world. The anger at the position she'd put him in. The deep acceptance that she'd been right in that moment, even if she'd been wrong in the end. Only now was he finally sure; what else could he do that would not risk too much?

"Confirm hibernation," he said. "Two thousand six hundred and twenty-nine years."

He would sleep, on and on until Sahia woke. Hopefully the settlement would prosper and there would be people there to welcome them. But if they woke in the empty husk of the ship, or not at all, it was a risk worth taking. He wondered if the settlers would work on the atmosphere until the sky tinged closer to sheer blue of Earth's, or if their factories might fill it with grey and choking smog before he woke, or some error might boil it from the planet so that he would wake once more beneath the blackness of space. In the end, it would not matter, for he knew that without Sahia there was no sky he could stand under and call that place his home.

See Will Gwaun's story "Mission and Submission" online at Metaphorosis.
If you liked it, leave a comment. Authors love that!
Remember to subscribe to our e-mail updates so you'll know when new stories are posted.

About the story

As with most of my stories, they seem to appear out of ideas sort of slamming together and producing a narrative. In the past these were usually pretty abstract and weird, ('What about the medieval catholic idea of itemised penance per mile of pilgrimage, combined with the technical problems of robots creating maps of their environments!?' is an example of something my brain will bother me with in the middle of the night, and then not leave me alone till I've written about it. See my very old story 'No S.L.A.M Maps for These Territories' for the result.) but recently they seem to be getting much more personal.

This one came about in the sort of emotional whiplash that followed finally finishing (after many false starts and near giving ups) my first novel after five years, and then not managing to sell it anywhere. I'm not under any illusion that I 'deserved' to sell it, after all you're competing with all the books ever written, plus the thousands of others from talented people arriving on editors' desks every month, and getting good at something usually takes more than one try, but it is a weird thing to pour all that work and effort into something and then just put it in a drawer. Writing seems unlike any other artistic endeavour in that way. At least with music or painting, even if you don't sell something you get to jam with your friends (or some other phrase that will make me sound less uncool) or hang it on your wall, but who has the time to read people's (probably often deservedly) unpublished novels, when there isn't the time to read all the amazing published novels that are in the world already?

Anyway, I was trying to find a way to express that feeling of sending bits of fiction you've poured all that work into out into the void of publishing, waiting for months (hats off to Metaphorosis for answering at what is practically lightspeed) and then receiving some form rejection.

At the same time, I was going through all the turmoil of working out of when it would make sense to start a family in the midst of trying to forge a career in a foreign country, and realising that this emphasis we have in our culture on 'never giving up on your dream' can be a pretty toxic thing for a lot of people, given the sacrifices it can mean. Finally, the of Boomer/Millennials/Gen-Z conflict narrative was starting to appear a lot online and in the media, which I found sort of alternately fascinating and depressing.

All of these things were sort of washing around in my head, and what fiction, especially speculative fiction, allows you to do is sort of cram all those ideas down into a single narrative thread, in a situation of heightened intensity, and then explore why that matters to the characters.

A question for the author

Q: Do you ever feel bad for what you put your characters through?

A: Hmm, not directly, no, but in a certain way, yes. I've heard some authors talk about how they 'have conversations with their characters' and so feel guilt for what happens to them, but this isn't something I really relate to.

There's that debate in cognitive science about whether we understand other people's mind through simulating in our own heads what it's like be them, or through forming theories about what they must be thinking. From my very layman's understanding of the debate, I feel like both of those things happen at different times, and different people seem to be inclined to engage in one mode more than the other. Most of the time that I'm writing, I feel like I'm much more in that 'theory' mode, trying to make sure that characters have motivations that make sense and act accordingly. Sometimes this leads to me sort of taking a perspective that isn't really my own, and with some stories that creates this feeling of 'wow, that would be a very bleak way of looking at the world'. To that extent, I do 'feel bad' for characters, and also there are moments when I get these sorts of flashes of empathy for the characters, where I can almost feel in my body what the emotions they're experiencing would be like (which I think of as being in 'simulation mode'). I think those moments have resulted in some of my favourite bits of writing, and in that way, I sometimes 'feel bad' in the sense that I briefly share in the misery/rage/despair I'm depicting, but not in not in the sense that I feel any responsibility for making them experience it.

I have a friend who's a TV writer, and he used to get hate mail all the time from fans for putting the characters through bad things. Complaints about gratuitous suffering would be something (and learning where the line is can be tricky), but they were really written as if he'd actually done that stuff to real people, and that seems pathological to me. Not to mention, suffering and struggle are indispensable to fiction and maybe to real life as well, but that's a bigger debate, and I've rambled enough.

About the author

Will comes from England but lives in Austria, where his struggles with the German language (and foolish instinct to just politely agree whenever he hasn't understood something) have a way of turning even mundane encounters into adventures in the surreal. He works as a teacher, physical therapist, and content writer. He likes to spend time in the woods and mountains, but seems to spend more of it sprawled on the sofa trawling nonsense on the internet.

@Wgwaun

The Future in a Wash Basin

Erin Keating

Co. Cork, 1896

Siobhan O'Keeffe Mahoney had never seen her own reflection. It was not for lack of trying. She would pass the only mirror in the house she shared with her father and brother, then quickly turn around, as though she could surprise it into revealing her image. She would stare so long into the gray waters of Schull Harbor on a windless day that, once, one of the rotten neighborhood boys pushed her in. She'd floated, of course. She would press her nose to the long icicles that formed beside their door in January, hoping for the briefest glimpse of the sea blue eyes and coppery hair she had inherited from her mother. But never once had she seen her own reflection.

Instead, she saw the future.

And from Siobhan's place in the worn armchair by the hearth, the future looked bleak.

Finn MacCotter stood opposite her, wringing his cap in his hands. She had understood all of the words Finn had said individually, but couldn't make sense of them in the order in which he had delivered them.

Siobhan wiped her clammy palms on her skirt. "I'm sorry, Mr. MacCotter. Am I correct that this is a proposal of marriage?"

Finn MacCotter glanced over his shoulder, where Siobhan's father, Cormac Mahoney, stood with his arms crossed.

"I certainly hope you're not sorry to hear it." He let out a wheezy laugh, and his freckled cheeks flushed. "My Da, eh, you know he's not well. He wants to see me, eh, settled. And he and Mr. Mahoney being such good friends and all—"

Siobhan's father cleared his throat. Finn stopped talking.

Siobhan supposed she shouldn't be surprised. She was newly twenty-two and

Finn a few years older, but it felt like there were fewer people their age in Schull Harbor by the hour—all packing their bags for America. Siobhan's stomach churned at the mere thought. How could they leave the only home that they knew for a place full of strangers?

Siobhan glanced over Finn's shoulder at the gilded-frame mirror that hung above the hearth. The clear surface of the mirror rippled as she looked at it. Should she marry Finn MacCotter or refuse? Each time she wavered, a misty image bubbled to the surface. That was what she loved most about the future—it was never set. Time ran steadily, like a river, and every decision she made took her down a different route of its forking path.

Siobhan saw herself scrubbing cow dung off Finn MacCotter's boots if she accepted or scrubbing her brother's children's dirty nappies if she refused. She would wash butchered blood from the cracks in Finn's leather gloves, or she would wash the blood from her sister-in-law's bedsheets after another birth. She would stare at the ceiling waiting for Finn to finish laboring over her in bed, or she would stare at the ceiling in the attic, displaced from her room, praying her screaming nieces and nephews would fall asleep.

Siobhan gripped the armchair with white knuckles. Her fingernails sank into the worn fabric. Was this it, then? Was she trapped by two tiresome fates—the obedient wife or the spinster aunt—without anything to call her own?

But then the image shifted to reveal a blonde daughter swaddled in Finn's arms. Siobhan nearly leapt from the armchair, her heart in her throat. If she took this path with Finn, she would have a daughter. Her mother's line would continue.

Siobhan blinked herself back to the present, to this worn armchair. She managed a smile. "Well, Mr. MacCotter, your proposal is certainly as good as any."

"Lovely! Eh, thank you. I'll, eh, go tell my Da." Finn MacCotter placed the wrung-out cap on his head. As soon as the front door closed, her brother and sister-in-law rushed in from the kitchen. They offered their congratulations, her sister-in-law trying awkwardly to embrace Siobhan around her own swollen belly.

Siobhan looked at her father, but he was studying the mirror closely, as he always did when he caught her scrying, wondering what secrets it revealed to his daughter.

That night, after some revelry with the neighbors, Siobhan put on her wool jacket, took an oil lantern from the hook by the door, and headed out into the dark. The late-March air cooled her flushed cheeks, warm with whiskey and the heat of a dozen bodies cramped in their small front room. The oil lantern lit only a small patch of road in front of her. It didn't matter. Her bones knew the way. She trod down Colla Road, away from the yellow, blue, and plum-colored houses of the main street. Between the trees and the shore scrub she could spy the inky water of the harbor and the lone light of a ship.

Soon, she came upon the cemetery. It sat beside the ruins of Saint Mary's Church, a roofless stone structure overgrown with shrubbery and moss. The old gate squeaked as she entered. Two matching headstones on freshly weeded plots sat at the base of the hill, overlooking the harbor. Siobhan settled down in the grass, leaning against her mother's cold stone.

"Ma, Gran, I'm getting married," she whispered.

And somewhere, far away or very near, Bridget O'Keeffe Mahoney and Emer Sullivan O'Keeffe listened. Siobhan felt heat flickering behind her navel—her magic. When she was a girl, she'd felt it strongest in Gran's kitchen, watching the old woman grinding herbs into healing salves. But in the years since Gran's death, it felt strongest here.

This was the land where her mother and her gran had practiced their craft. This was the land where her own daughters would learn their arts. Even though the town seemed to be growing smaller each day, she couldn't bear to leave Schull Harbor and the bones of the women who came before her. This land was her inheritance.

She pressed her fingers to the earth and spoke the Old Irish word for 'water'. It was a tongue lost to nearly all but the wise women, a language she had learned from her gran. The ground yielded to her touch, and soon fresh water bubbled up and pooled at the base of the stones. She would use the water's surface to scry.

She had chosen the path in which she would bear children—even if they were

Finn MacCotter's children. Her mother's line would continue. Her daughter would learn magic at her elbow.

Siobhan whispered, "Show me my line."

The surface of the water rippled, revealing the image of a blonde little girl. The child hid behind Finn's legs, his arms stretched out in front of her—shielding her from something. In this vision, Siobhan reached for her daughter, but the girl and Finn both backed away. They looked afraid—afraid of her.

Siobhan sank her fingers into the dirt, felt the comforting hum of her foremother's magic.

"Again," she demanded of the water through gritted teeth.

The next vision had the same blonde girl studying a children's catechism in the MacCotter's large parlor. The view was at a strange angle, but then the vision grew wider until Siobhan saw herself peering through a crack in the doorway. Then Finn appeared, his mouth in a tight line, and closed the door.

"No," Siobhan gasped. She could hardly breathe over the lump forming in her throat. "No, no, no."

She sank her hands into the pool of water, splashing away the vision. "Please, do any of them practice?" she begged. "Do any of them scry?"

The water grew cloudy with mud and when it settled, the image of three copper-haired girls flashed in quick succession.

Then, for the first time in Siobhan's life, she thought she saw her reflection. A sea blue eye stared back at her, too close to the surface of the water.

It blinked.

Siobhan, startled, tumbled backward into the grass. But she crept forward again, and peered into the pool. The face pulled away from the water's surface, revealing the girl's other eye, a pert freckle-dusted nose, and a crooked smile with new teeth growing in awkwardly.

"Hi!" The girl said. Her face rippled as a gentle breeze skirted across the surface of the water. Her voice was strange, an accent with sharp, narrow sounds that grated Siobhan's ears.

"Hello," Siobhan said cautiously. Often, she could hear the scenes that she scried, but she had never been able to communicate with them. Something about this seemed touched with fae magic.

"Do you see funny things in the mirror too?" the girl asked.

"I do," Siobhan answered.

"Have you ever seen yourself?"

"No."

"Me either." The girl shrugged. "What did you ask the mirror to see? Oh, I guess you aren't using a mirror, are you? You're all—wavy."

Siobhan laughed, the sound so loud in the silent night that she scared herself. This girl spoke so many words, and so quickly. The flame in Siobhan's stomach grew hotter, white heat rippling through her body. It was a powerful feeling, a prideful and protective affection. She hadn't expected to feel it this suddenly. Perhaps it was because she knelt on her mother's and gran's graves—a heritage of blood and bones. This was a girl of her line.

"I asked to see my family," Siobhan said.

The girl grinned, lips parting to reveal her lopsided teeth again. "You're Siobhan, aren't you?" Siobhan must have made a surprised face, because the girl laughed. "My mom's told me all about you—you're her great-grandma—I think. I'm Bridget! It's nice to meet you."

Siobhan caught her breath hearing her mother's name spoken in the girl's strange voice.

"Tell me about your mother," Siobhan whispered.

She listened to Bridget tell her about her mother, who was attuned to stones and crystals, who used citrine to manifest enough cash to make ends meet, rose quartz to ease her broken heart after Bridget's father left, amethyst under Bridget's pillow to keep bad dreams away.

Hearing the stories reminded Siobhan of the tales she'd heard of her own mother, who could press her hands to a stone and hear its history.

As the moon rose and set, the water slowly dried up. Siobhan finally said goodbye to Bridget—this scried girl with her mother's name—who stared up at her through the water. When Bridget's image was gone, and Siobhan was alone in the cemetery once more, she whispered a prayer of thanks over the graves. Her line would go on.

But she couldn't shake the image of her blonde daughter's wide blue eyes and trembling mouth. What could make a child look at her mother like that?

The next day, Siobhan and her father donned their Sunday best and walked down the long dirt road toward MacCotter's Farm. The cows in the pasture lumbered up to them, stretching their heads over the low stone walls as though to inspect Siobhan personally. Milk, cheese, butter, and the highest quality meat came out of MacCotter's Farm. At least a dozen men in town were employed there as farmhands—those who did not go to sea every day, as Siobhan's father did.

The morning damp clung to Siobhan's skin. Her cheeks stung with cold when they finally reached the MacCotter's stone house. Finn MacCotter answered the door, smartly dressed, with his curly blond hair parted and beard newly trimmed.

"Welcome, eh, if you'll follow me this way."

"Is that them?" A voice called from the other room.

"Yes, Da!" Finn shouted back.

Finn led them into the foyer. Siobhan had been inside the MacCotters' house before—they held an annual Christmas party for the whole town—but she hadn't expected it to look so splendid on an ordinary day. The dark wooden banisters gleamed. She followed the stairs with her eyes, generations of blond MacCotters looking down on her from oil portraits. To their right was a large formal dining room, where the MacCotters hosted Christmas dinner at a table laden with silver. To their left was a dimly lit parlor that was twice the size of the Mahoney's front room. There Mr. MacCotter sat in a chair by a roaring fire, wrapped in blankets.

Despite the grandeur, a chill shuddered down Siobhan's back. Without the bustle of the Christmas guests, an eerie quiet sat heavily on the house.

"Cormac, welcome! And Miss Mahoney, come here, come here." Siobhan allowed Mr. MacCotter to kiss her hand.

"Finbarr!" Mr. Mahoney boomed, shaking Mr. MacCotter's liver-spotted hand. "All's well with the farm?"

Though they were the same age, Mr. MacCotter seemed decades older than his friend, stooped and hunched with pain no one could cure. Perhaps Gran O'Keeffe could have healed him, had he fallen ill in her time.

"Fine, fine," Mr. MacCotter wheezed. "Except I don't know how I'll keep staffing it. America is stealing all my farmhands' sons. It seems a man can't expect his children to stay in one place anymore. We must be the luckiest men in all of Cork."

Siobhan glanced at Finn, who stood stiffly beside his father, his eyes fixed to a spot on the floor. Had he ever dreamed of leaving for America, like so many others? Or was he like her—proud to be tied to this land and his family's history here?

Mr. MacCotter cleared his throat with a phlegmy rattle in his chest. "Now, Miss Mahoney, let me look at you."

Siobhan wore a dress of carnation red, a fawn-colored wool shawl embroidered with rosebuds, and her coppery hair neatly pinned. Of course, there had been no way for her to see how she looked. But, that morning, as she peered into her wash basin, Bridget's face had appeared.

Bridget was older than she'd been when they'd spoken in the cemetery—now a woman in her sixties with elegant white hair. Bridget had said that Siobhan looked beautiful. That was better than any reflection.

"Turn please," Mr. MacCotter said. Siobhan gave a girlish twirl and Mr. MacCotter let out an annoyed sound like a cow's loam. "No, girl, slowly, please, slowly."

So, Siobhan turned slowly in a full circle, feeling the weight of the men's eyes on her. She tried to make a face to her father, but his arms were crossed, watching Mr. MacCotter closely.

"Very good. Now, if you would please smile," Mr. MacCotter instructed.

Siobhan did her best lady-like smile, demure and closed-lipped. Again, a cow-like sound burst from Mr. MacCotter, sending spittle flying. "No, girl—your teeth. I want to see your teeth."

Siobhan realized that she was not a woman, trying to impress her father-in-law, but a cow being inspected at auction. She bared her teeth, curling her lips as far back as she could manage.

"Siobhan!" her father hissed.

But Mr. MacCotter didn't seem to notice the gesture. "She's looks healthy, and any daughter of yours must have a strong constitution. Her hips—wideset—good for child-bearing. We'd hate to see her go the way of her mother."

A flame sparked in the pit of Siobhan's stomach, equal parts magic and rage.

Siobhan tried to keep her voice level. "There was nothing wrong with my mother."

"Siobhan, now is not the time," her father warned, his voice low.

"Of course, my girl, of course. If your kind father had insisted the doctor be present for the whole labor instead of leaving it up to his addled mother-in-law, perhaps she would have made it," Mr. MacCotter said.

Fire spread through Siobhan's core, heat moving up into her chest. Frost began to spread on the windowpane as she balled her fists. She muttered the Old Irish word for 'breath', trying her gran's old trick for calming a racing heart.

"What was that, girl?" Mr. MacCotter demanded. The word 'girl' chafed at her skin.

The frost grew with a low cracking. Siobhan snapped. "If my father hadn't called for the doctor at the last minute and had let my gran continue her treatment, my mother most certainly would have made it."

Gran O'Keeffe had told her the story. Her father, in his terror, called for the doctor, who had thrown Gran O'Keeffe from the room. She had finished brewing ergot tea—a thimbleful of ergot powder brewed in boiling water—that would make her mother's uterine muscles contract and stop the bleeding. The doctor had knocked the teacup from her hand, convinced ergot was poisonous. He packed Bridget O'Keeffe Mahoney full of cotton, which she bled through, and bled through, and bled through, while the tea that could have saved her seeped into the floorboards. Gran O'Keeffe rocked Siobhan, newly born and wailing, outside the door while her daughter died.

"I said not now, Siobhan!" her father snapped.

The thick ice on the window shone like silver. And in it, Siobhan saw herself in labor, her face red with sweat, screaming in primal pain. When the child arrived in the world, Finn snatched it from her arms, as though Siobhan was diseased.

She squeezed her eyes shut, willing the image away.

"There, there, my girl. I did not mean to upset you. Of course, you miss your mother at a time like this," Mr. MacCotter said.

In truth, Siobhan rarely missed her mother, though she would never dare say that aloud in front of her father. There was no need to miss her; her presence was constant. Every time she felt her magic tug at her stomach, it was like her mother was there beside her. But in this house, with its too-dark and too-quiet rooms, lorded over by Mr. MacCotter and his ever-watchful gaze, could she practice safely here?

Mr. MacCotter squeezed her hand, and Siobhan fought the urge to pull away.

Panic flickered and flared in her chest like a dying candle. These men would snuff her out.

Hours later, Siobhan had rubbed her skin red and raw, but still could not shake the chill of the MacCotters' house. She had locked the door of her little room with its drafty window that overlooked the harbor. Despite her sister-in-law's incessant knocking, Siobhan didn't answer. She tried to lose herself in the rhythm of the squeaking floorboards as she paced. Only when her feet had grown tired did she pour some water into the basin by her bed.

"Show me Bridget," she demanded. The surface of the water rippled, and Bridget's face came into view. She was younger than she had been when they spoke that morning, when she complimented

Siobhan's dress. Now a woman in her early thirties, the only wrinkles on Bridget's face were faint laugh lines around her mouth.

Siobhan was sure that Bridget was aging normally in her own time, growing a little older each day. But the mirror carried Bridget back from different parts of her life to this point in Siobhan's. This point was an anchor, a moment of significance, that had affected the fate of Siobhan's line. Siobhan took comfort in this—it was a sign that her marriage to Finn MacCotter would not be for nothing, despite her unsettling visions and his father's frigid, suffocating house.

"Oh! Siobhan! Hi!" Bridget chirped. Her energy never changed—whether she was a girl or a woman or an old lady. She always spoke so fast, Siobhan could hardly understand her. "I'm glad to see you. I've got big news actually, something I think you'd really like to know."

"Go on, my heart," Siobhan said. Even though Bridget appeared older than her now, she was still overwhelmed by a warm rush of affection. There was a maternal fondness for Bridget that Siobhan could not shake, despite the years that separated them.

"I'm pregnant! You're the first person other than my husband to know—weird, right?" Light radiated from Bridget's dewy cheeks. "It's going to be a girl—I just know it."

Siobhan's throat felt tight. Echoing through her head were her own screams of labor that she had scried in the MacCotters' windows.

"Congratulations—that is..." Siobhan murmured. She recalled Gran's story of her birth and her mother's death—the two tangled up together. She clutched the ceramic basin, pressing it into her stomach as a wave of nausea passed over her. As much as Siobhan wanted a daughter, childbirth itself was a nightmare that had haunted her all her life. And to think that Bridget would soon go through it, wherever and whenever she was.

"Are you all right?" Bridget asked. Two deep worry lines creased her forehead.

Siobhan nodded. "My mother..." was all she could manage.

"Shit!" Bridget hissed. "I'm so sorry. Mom told me about your mother. Of course, you're concerned. But I'll be all right, I promise."

Siobhan thought of her conversation with Bridget just this morning. Bridget would live to have crow's feet around her eyes and sleek white hair.

"I know you will, my heart," Siobhan said. Then she swallowed hard, trying to speak through the lump in her throat. "Bridget, do you know if our magic skipped over someone in our line. Did your mom's grandma practice?"

Bridget began to laugh, but caught herself. Siobhan wondered how worry wrote itself on her face—did she have the same deep worry lines as her great-great-granddaughter? "She must have—I've heard stories from my grandma that she was a healer. Why do you ask?"

Siobhan clutched at her stomach. Bridget's words didn't seem to align with her visions at all. "What about when she was young? How did her gift grow?"

Bridget tilted her head. "Siobhan, you already know the answer. Our magic can only grow if we practice it."

The wedding was set for August. Though the date was months away, there was already a flurry of preparation at the

Mahoney house. Her sister-in-law and three of Mr. Mahoney's sisters took it upon themselves to tailor Siobhan's mother's wedding dress for the occasion. She could never seem to breathe in her wedding dress, no matter how many times they let it out.

There were arguments over what they should serve at the Mahoney's house following the ceremony, which readings would be best for the mass, whether foxglove or iris would look prettier in a bouquet. Siobhan was seldom asked for her opinion, so she chose not to offer it. Instead, she stood quietly on an overturned soap box, letting herself be pricked with pins, as her mind raced.

The problem had to be Finn. In every vision she'd have of her blonde daughter—Finn's daughter—he stood between them. She had to convince him that their child needed to practice her craft, that this was Siobhan's legacy. She could not let her daughter's magic die.

Whenever one of the aunts held up a mirror for Siobhan to inspect their progress, Siobhan saw the image of her daughter with Finn, with terror in her blue eyes, pulling away from Siobhan.

She breathed deeply until her ribs strained against the seams, and she tugged at the lace against her sweaty neck. The aunts tutted and pinned some more, but Siobhan's dry mouth couldn't form the words to tell them that the problem wasn't the dress—it was her future.

One day, a month into wedding preparations, when the aunts gossiped about a neighbor's daughter leaving for America, Finn MacCotter knocked on the door. The Mahoney women fussed like hens as they barred Finn from entering until Siobhan changed out of her wedding gown.

"Sorry for the trouble," Siobhan said when she finally let him in. She tried to smile at him, but felt more like a wolf bearing its fangs. Each time she saw him, she searched his eyes for the disgust she had seen in her visions. A steady fury, like waves beating against the coast, built up in her for all of the things he had yet to do.

"No trouble. But I have, eh, some news. Well, a request really." Finn removed his cap, wringing it in his hands. "My Da, eh, took a turn. I know there's so much to do, and, eh, I don't want to burden your family. But, do you think we could move up the date?" Finn asked. "To next week?"

Siobhan's stomach clenched so suddenly she thought she'd be sick on Finn's shoes. She'd expected a couple more months to find a way to convince him that she—and their future daughter—needed to be able to practice their craft. But next week? She leaned against the door to steady herself. "I'm not sure. I—"

But then her sister-in-law and the aunts burst from the kitchen where they'd been eavesdropping. "Not a burden at all," her sister-in-law said. "We can manage."

At those words, the mounting fear turned to flame. It started behind Siobhan's navel and spread outward until her fingertips burned. The air around her rippled with heat. She worried that the house would catch fire if she didn't do something. Siobhan cast her gaze toward the harbor.

"Finn, come with me." She grabbed him by the elbow, but Finn yelped in pain and leapt away. His shirt had been scorched.

Siobhan didn't apologize or explain. Instead, she walked out into the bright

May morning. His heavy footsteps followed. Only when they were halfway to the harbor, far from her sister-in-law's uncanny hearing, did Siobhan dare to speak.

"Finn, you know what I am, don't you?"

"What do you—" he began.

"Please," she interrupted. "It's a small town. You know the rumors. You know my gran was a wise-woman. You know that I—well—I see things." The fire of her magic grew hotter in the pit of her stomach, as though by speaking it she had fed the flames. She felt her power rippling off her skin. Down the road, the harbor waters grew mirror-still.

Finn tugged at his shirt collar. His neck and cheeks turned splotchy red. "I've heard. But, eh, I'm willing to look past it. We'll have an ordinary life."

"Ordinary?" Siobhan felt the air rush from her lungs.

"Ordinary. We'll run a good house, and raise good children, and no one will say that you're odd."

"What about our daughter? If she sees things too?" Rage and fear were a potent combination for women with her gift. It was like adding whiskey to a flame. Her power flared up, casting a glassy frost across all of the neighbors' windows.

"There's no need to encourage her—abilities. She'll be ordinary, like any other child. What more could she want?" He reached out to hold her hand, but pulled back. "What more could you want?"

"I want her to inherit what is hers." She held Finn's gaze. Long silence hung between them, interrupted only by the sound of groaning ice.

"MacCotter Farm will be her inheritance, if we have no sons." His voice sounded hollow, like the vast rooms of his father's house. "And we are done with this discussion."

He turned away from her, but, just before he did, she saw in his eyes what she had been searching for, for weeks. Disgust. Anger. A shadow of fear.

This was the Finn MacCotter of her visions, the one who shielded her own daughter from her, who banished magic from their home, who cast Siobhan into loneliness. This was not the life she had chosen when she accepted his proposal.

The fire of her magic roared inside her. All of the power that she'd stoked released in a rush. A sudden frost descended on the streets of Schull Harbor, the town encased in a mirrored sheen of ice. And in it, Siobhan finally understood her visions.

On the icy road ahead of her, heading back toward her father's house, she saw the blonde daughter and her fearful eyes. On the road leading down to the harbor, she saw a copper-haired girl, reading in Siobhan's lap.

Siobhan laughed aloud and, with it, icicles crashed to the ground.

How had she forgotten? In her panic at her line dying, she had forgotten the simple truth. The future was not fixed. That blonde-haired daughter she had seen was only one possible child that would come to be—Finn's child. But she remembered the line of copper-haired girls she had first scried in the puddle at the cemetery—those were the daughters of a life and a love yet unknown to her.

Siobhan raced back to her father's house, ignoring the frantic questioning of her aunts and sister-in-law. In her room, she dragged her wardrobe in front of her door, straining and sweating under the effort. She didn't know how long she'd have until her father found out about her fight with Finn. And she needed time to think.

She filled her wash basin, splashing half of the pitcher on the floor with her shaking hands. "What should I do?" she begged of the water.

The water rippled and bubbled, showing her glimpses of every possible future. She could marry Finn MacCotter and have their miserable, magicless daughter. She could stay in Schull Harbor, unmarried, tending the graves of Ma and Gran. She could take the path that traveled past the curve in the coastline that had marked the edge of Siobhan's whole world. Limitless possibilities danced across the water's surface until Siobhan grew dizzy.

She gripped the ceramic basin to steady herself. "Stop," she hissed. The water stilled. She should have known better than to ask the water such an open-ended the question. It could only show her the paths—it could not tell her what to do.

Downstairs, the door slammed. The whole house seemed to rock as her father stormed in.

"Show me Bridget," she demanded. Her voice was tight in her throat. She didn't have much time.

The water rippled, and then Bridget was looking up at her. She was a young woman, nearly Siobhan's age. Her sea blue eyes were watery and red-rimmed, and her coppery hair was disheveled. A few hair pins still clung to her curls. At the edge of the basin, Siobhan glimpsed the neckline of a black dress.

Siobhan's fevered thoughts stilled. Her chest ached as she studied her great-great-granddaughter's quivering chin.

"Oh, my heart, what happened? What's wrong?" Siobhan murmured.

"My grandma—she—" Bridget wiped her eyes. "Could you—could you tell me about yours?" she asked.

But then there was a pounding at the door.

"Siobhan—Siobhan, open this door this instant," her father roared.

"Siobhan, is everything all right?" Bridget asked, drying her eyes.

"Everything is fine, my heart. Don't worry about a thing," Siobhan murmured.

"Finn MacCotter is down at the harbor calling you a—he was calling you a..."

Even after all these years, her father still couldn't bring himself to say it.

Siobhan whispered the Old Irish word for 'quiet'. The room stopped rattling, her father stopped thundering. A thick blanket of silence had fallen over everything except Siobhan and her wash basin. Bridget needed her, and Siobhan would let nothing interrupt them.

Siobhan sighed, returning her attention to Bridget. "You wanted to hear about Gran O'Keefe, yes?"

Bridget nodded, her red-rimmed eyes wide with surprise.

Gran O'Keeffe had been Siobhan's whole heritage—serving as both grandmother and mother. The air around Siobhan crackled with Gran O'Keeffe's memory. Since Gran's death, there was a word Siobhan hadn't spoken. But Bridget deserved to hear it.

"My Gran O'Keeffe was a witch, like us."

Gran O'Keeffe was the one who named Siobhan's ability. Scrying: that was the word for seeing the future in the mirror, in water, in ice. Any witch worth her salt could learn to scry, but only once in several generations was a witch born a natural scryer. Gran O'Keeffe's own mother had been one. It had been enough, to see the look of pride on Gran O'Keeffe's face, rather than ever seeing her own.

In this very house, Siobhan had learned the healing arts at Gran's elbow—borage seed oil for aching bones, honeyed marshmallow root for cough, yarrow tea for fevers. Though the plants would not speak to Siobhan as they had to Gran O'Keefe, it had been enough to feel the heat of their shared magic ripple through the small kitchen as old and young woman worked side by side.

In this very room, Gran O'Keefe had brushed and braided Siobhan's copper hair, describing the face that had eluded Siobhan all her life. "You look just like your ma did at this age," Gran O'Keefe would whisper as she worked her knobby fingers through Siobhan's hair. "Big eyes as blue as the sky."

Schull Harbor was her home, where memories of Gran O'Keefe were embedded into the grains of the wooden house and the cracks of the cobblestone streets. Schull Harbor was all she had known, and she loved it—despite its smallness that only got smaller—because it was here that she had learned her craft. This town was all she was. Could she really leave it all behind? Leave Ma and Gran O'Keefe's bones, their memories?

Siobhan watched the lines of grief ease on Bridget's face as she spoke. Siobhan didn't care how many generations stood between her and her daughter's, daughter's, daughter's daughter. Bridget was flesh of her flesh and blood of her blood. She loved her as though she had carried her herself—as Gran O'Keefe had loved Siobhan.

Gran O'Keefe would understand.

Siobhan realized then that she did not need the water to tell her what to do. There were hundreds of paths that could lead to copper-haired daughters learning their craft. But she wanted just one path —she wanted the future that led to Bridget.

Her magic smoldered in her stomach. That tugging, fiery sensation behind her navel burned brighter than it had in years. Siobhan had always thought that her power came from this land, from the buried bones of her foremothers. But as she watched her great-great-granddaughter's face—the one she has seen age in the rippling waters of her wash basin—she understood the truth.

Their magic was not tied to the land. Their magic was tied to each other.

These abilities were her inheritance and her legacy—hers to remember and hers to leave behind. This young woman who scried the past while Siobhan scried the future was proof of that legacy.

"You come from a long line of extraordinary women." Siobhan's voice crackled with power.

With those words, the wash basin in her hands turned to crystal. The surface of the water stilled into silver glass. The future itself turned solid and clear.

"Bridget," she asked her great-great-granddaughter, "where are you?"

Bridget grinned, because she had known this future all along. "Brooklyn."

"Brooklyn." The word fell from Siobhan's lips like an irreversible spell. It was a place that sounded too big for her wash basin, so Siobhan threw open the window. "Show me," she demanded of the harbor. The blistering heat under her skin seeped out of her, until the air around her hummed. The harbor turned to solid ice—boats were trapped, fisherman's frozen nets were too heavy to pull, children splashing in the shallows skated along a sheen of glass.

Siobhan feared the ice would show her the future of Schull Harbor with wild grass growing over her foremothers' graves. But it didn't. Instead, she witnessed her own line stretch for generations beyond the harbor and across the Atlantic. Tears streamed down Siobhan's cheeks. In those faces, she saw Ma's blue eyes and Gran's knowing smile repeated and changed like an old incantation.

Siobhan tore away from the window to peer back into the crystal basin. Bridget raised her eyebrows, as though to ask Siobhan what she had seen, even though she already knew. How Siobhan loved her, this girl of her line.

"My heart," Siobhan breathed. "I'm on my way."

See Erin Keating's story "The Future in a Wash Basin" online at Metaphorosis.
If you liked it, leave a comment. Authors love that!
Remember to subscribe to our e-mail updates so you'll know when new stories are posted.

About the story

"The Future in a Wash Basin" began at the end.

When I'm coming up with ideas for stories, I tend to think of interesting or unusual images that I can build a character and a world around. For this story, that image was of a woman scrying in a compact mirror. From there I worked backward, trying to figure out who this woman was and what she saw in the mirror. At first, I liked the idea of telling multiple connected stories about an entire lineage of women, each one scrying into a different object—but as I explored that idea, it quickly grew out-of-hand for a short story.

Instead, I traced the story back to the matriarch and decided to begin there. Once I decided to focus the story on Siobhan, the plot fell into place. I knew that I wanted to center the story around a specific moment in Siobhan's life that would affect the fate of the rest of her line and which could be grounded in a real, historical moment. In the early drafts of this story, the final scene jumped ahead to the perspective of Bridget—Siobhan's   great-great-granddaughter— scrying into a compact mirror and looking back into the past.

Metaphorosis's editor, B. Morris Allen, requested a rewrite of the story, which led to me re-imagining the way Siobhan's visions worked. Because I began at the end, Siobhan's choice had felt inevitable and her visions pointed to one future. During my revisions, I worked to show that multiple paths diverged from her decision. In doing so, I also ended up cutting that final scene from Bridget's perspective, so that the piece had a clear focus on Siobhan. These revisions helped me hone in on this crucial moment for Siobhan where her heritage and her legacy intersect.

In the end, this story was inspired by an image that didn't make it into the final version. That just means that I have another story to tell! While I figure out exactly what Bridget is scrying in her compact mirror, I hope that you enjoy "The Future in a Wash Basin."

A question for the author

Q: Q: Do you write things other than speculative fiction?

A: I do! While writing fiction—especially speculative fiction—always feels most natural to me, the first formal creative writing instruction I received was in poetry. The attention to sound and the specificity of word choice that's required in poetry is something that I try to practice when revising my fiction. Whenever I'm feeling stuck on a story, I find that writing a short poem is the best way to get me focused on the fundamentals of craft.

Poetry and fiction tend to feel like very independent endeavors, so every now and then I like to explore more collaborative forms. I find playwriting particularly exciting, because the piece really only comes to life when the actors add their own voices to it. My senior year of college, I wrote and directed a full-length play about the heroines of Shakespeare's three Verona plays (*Taming Of The Shrew, Romeo And Juliet,* and *Two Gentlemen Of Verona*).

Most recently, I've been trying my hand at songwriting. My husband is a musician and we've been passing pieces back and forth—I'll give him lyrics to set music to, and he'll give me music to add words to. It's been a really fun process!

About the author

Erin Keating is a grant writer at an arts education nonprofit. She earned her B.A. in creative writing and literature at Roanoke College. While earning her history M.A. at Drew University, she spent most of her time in the archives reading as many Shakespeare-related texts she could find. She has a library card from the Bodleian Library, Library of Congress, Folger Shakespeare Library, and, of course, her local public library. When she's not writing, she dabbles in bass guitar, rock climbing, language-learning, and video games.

erinkeatingwrites.com, @KeatingNotKeats

The Year of the Bright Lands

Felix Taylor

The Year of the Anabatic Wind was coming to an end. Everything had happened as it should have done, every prophecy made by the Under Personage, the Great Ancestor of the Pit, had come to pass. All except for the Wind itself. There had been no sign of it, no rush of warm air over the fields, no whisper of it blowing in the flatlands away to the north. I could not help but think that it was all my fault.

I had always considered my dreams too dull to give to the diviner for interpretation. They were the kind that everyone had, and their meanings were plain. The building of a house — that meant that I yearned for a proper home and a good husband. Walking along a road — that meant that I was on the path that had been set out for me by the Personage during the Nights of First Becoming. Dull, all of them. Except for the dream I'd had in the final month of the Year of Unsowing, two years ago. In that dream, I flung myself bodily into the Abyss and my heart squeezed against my throat, beating waves of white heat into my arms as I dropped. Cold wind cut my face.

When the archivists had read aloud from the prophecies at the next year's beginning, I almost choked.

"She will be in black dress," they had said, "in imitation of the soul which is absent of light. Before winter's end she will hurl herself into the Pit and come to the light of the stars and be reborn in the Ancestor's image. So commences the Year of Resplendent Sacrifice, foretold by the Under Personage, the Giver of Night."

We all looked around at each other, gathered before the doors of the Archive, wondering which of us would be the chosen girl. I had been scared. The flames from the lamps twisted the other girls' faces, hollowed out their eyes, brightened their teeth. *It's me*, I said to myself, *because I have seen it.* We looked at each other and I knew that every pair of eyes had landed on me, whipping away before I'd noticed. Perhaps they'd all seen me fall in their own dreams. Perhaps my fear showed like a pimple on my nose or a rash which crept across my forehead.

"For only in light," the assistant archivist had continued, her arms glittering from circlets of black gemstones, "can a soul be unmade and there return to its maker in darkness."

The Year of Resplendent Sacrifice had approached its end and no one had jumped. During eighth month, Demira Sinter, a girl who lived next to us in a house with three floors, approached the Abyss and stared down into its darkness. We crept along behind her, darting from rock to furrow, wondering if Demira would be the one to do it, but she plodded back to the village without a word and shut herself in her bedroom. And then, on the final day, a woman who lived alone named Clara Reed put on a black bathing robe and, shrieking to herself, leapt into the Night to join the Personage. She had been of middling age, only some years younger than Mother —not a girl by any standard.

But the archivists declared the prophecy to have been fulfilled and we let the Year of Resplendent Sacrifice fall from our memories.

The following year, the corn grew seven inches in the first quarter. Three juniper birds were seen at the appearance of the Bright Scar, and a father of two boys was lost while out gathering white mushrooms in the flats. All just as it should have occurred. And again: 'But where is the Wind?' People began to worry. My mother asked it at the start of each morning, and by evening's close she had fretted herself to the point of sickness. The anticipation across the rest of our community was so unbearable that by the end of the year, every gust of warm air from the Abyss was proclaimed to be the beginnings of the Anabatic Wind and we gathered at the fields' edge to await — what? Something. Anything would have been better than that stillness. For a moment, the sweet grasses around our ankles might shiver and shake and the archivists would stand eager to record the Great Event, only for their pens to fall to their sides, their parchment to hang limp in their disappointed grips.

"One thousand years," I heard the assistant archivist Janny Lin murmur to a colleague. We were walking back to the village after one of these false alarms. "One thousand years and before tonight only a single prophecy has not unfolded."

"What was supposed to happen?" I asked, moving to walk beside Janny and the other archivists. Pendants of black slate swung from their wrists, their badges of office.

Janny narrowed her eyes and squinted ahead as if she had not heard my question. "A ball of flame," she said. "It was meant to appear as the Bright Scar opened. So it was foretold."

"A candle flame?" I ventured, though I knew what she would say.

"Greater than that." Janny's eyes flicked over to me and away. "A *sun*, the Under Personage called it."

I had heard of suns before, but only in tales passed around by the boys who worked at the outer edges of the village. There were places, they said, where days were counted by the movements of great circles of light, and that the light of one of them was brighter even than the wood fire in the village hall. The people there had no knowledge of the Ancestor and no notion of who they were in the world. They had their sun and that was all that they ever thought they needed. I never liked to imagine those places.

"But it didn't appear?" I asked Janny Lin.

"The Year of the Life Star, it was called. Our eight hundred and first year. No event like it was recorded by the archivists. No ball of flame. Nothing."

"But what about last year?" said a shadow to Janny's right. Her colleague, dressed in the same robes the colour of dusk. "If we are to count it. The girl did not jump, but a woman in her place."

"It is not well to speak too long about these things," said Janny.

I saw Mother watching me from a group of older women, her brow folded in disapproval. I nodded and drifted away from Janny Lin. *It is not well.* The Personage was the Voice of Truth in the Darkness. It was never wrong, *could* never be wrong. Infallible, the High Priest always said. Undeniable. Unreadable. Fifteen hundred years ago, the Abyss had spoken and the first men and women of our village had recorded the words. A map, the Priest said, of our entire existence, stretching out into the night, the undying darkness when starlight did not shine. It was why we worshiped at night and set great store by the dreamworld. We stayed within the boundaries of the flatlands, just as the Personage instructed, because beyond the flatlands lay the ends of life.

In the beginning there was the void, the High Priest said at the start of each mass. And the void did take form. It became a nest of snakes, and the snakes tried selfishly to fashion a world of light for themselves, but darkness swept up from the deeps and scattered them. Then came the Abyss. The Personage was everywhere, but especially in the Abyss.

The light from the stars had all but faded by the time we reached our homes. The day was at an end. Mother rushed straight to her seat by the window where she kept her collection of black quartz stones. They had been gathered from the very wall of the Abyss and were strictly contraband, but mother had traded six days of new sour milk for them and they had been a solace to her, a reassurance that she was at one with the Abyss and the Personage. I went to my bedroom, and eventually to sleep, and the Year of the Anabatic Wind passed unfulfilled.

The next morning, I woke with the first stars. I washed in cold water drawn up from the well and ate white bread with Mother in the kitchen. She was always up before me. She only slept for a few hours, she said; it was all she could manage these days. She couldn't listen to the sounds of the rafters in her bedroom creaking, because it put daggers in her head. I watched her from across the table and knew that she had been worrying about the Anabatic Wind.

"The year is over, Mama," I said.

"What will happen will happen," mother said, folding her hands.

"But there's no use dwelling," I said.

"There's use," she said sullenly. Like a child. Like me. "You're just like your pa, Elin. Pretending everything's as it should be when it is not."

"But nothing has changed," I went on. "The wind did not come, but things are the same as before."

"You need to understand," said mother. "That the word of the Personage is the world."

"I know that, Mama."

"And the prophecies are the truth of the world and of the village. If they do not come to pass, then it is we who are made false."

I got up and left before she thought to say anything else. *We who are made false.* Mother's words crawled into my ear like a beetle. They stayed as I rinsed the breakfast dishes and made ready for school. I was false, then. The dream had been a preparation for the year to come, a *revelation*, I knew it was called. And I had been too afraid.

The schoolhouse was across the square: I could see its lanterns glowing from our kitchen window. Beyond the schoolhouse lay the edges of the village and a place called the Den, where our wine was made. Boys and girls whose parents did not want them going to school were sent there to work. They were not usually seen this close to the square, but that morning, as I stepped out into the still air, I saw one of the boys sitting in the shadow of the fountain. Dirt plastered his face and his hair was tousled at odd angles, as if he'd been in a scrap. He might have only been two or three years younger than me. He stank, too, I thought, as I walked by the lights of the fountain.

I wouldn't have talked to him if he hadn't been crying. His lips quivered and tears glittered and fell from his face.

"You can't be lost, can you?" I asked, standing beside him.

His head shook and I heard a sniff.

"Not," he said.

"Then what's the matter?" I said.

The boy looked up at me and I saw confusion in his gaze.

"They boys from they Den," he said. "They stoled my waxy doll and threw it into yon Pit. Now it's there at they bottom."

"That's not kind of them," I said, frowning in sympathy. He spoke strangely, this boy. I'd never heard anything like it. "But there isn't a bottom of the Pit, you know."

I knew it was blasphemy for him to say it. The Abyss had no bounds, no limits that any person could comprehend, that's what the High Priest had taught us. There could be no bottom.

"So is too," the boy said, looking away now. "I'n been there and thrown a girt rock. Crack, it went in they water!"

"But there's no way down," I said. "That's what the adults say. And anyone who tries to find a way is breaking the

Will of the Personage. You couldn't have been down there because there's nowhere to go."

"Purse on edge," the boy mouthed.

"I know about those boys though," I said, deciding to show sympathy. "From the Den. My friends are always saying what mean things they do there."

"Will you go with me?" the boy said, standing up. A single tear shot down his cheek just like the Bright Scar.

"With you?" I asked. "To the Abyss?"

"Yes, missus," he said eagerly. "To they bottom."

"Can't your dad help you find your doll?" I asked.

"No'm," he blinked, and looked away. "I hain't seen my daddun for long."

"Where does he work?" I asked

"With they horsies."

I didn't know what that was.

"Can you come?" he asked.

"I can't," I said, deciding not to argue with him any longer. "I'm sorry. If they did throw your wax doll down, there's no way to get it back."

The boy was still there when I came out from our morning lesson an hour later. He was there again after I'd seen in the milking. He had draped himself over the rim of the fountain, cradling his forehead with his wrists. He was a naïve little boy, I thought, and his father should know better than to fill his head with lies about the Abyss. There *was* no bottom. There was no other side, either, nothing but the presence of the Personage, which, I knew, was also nothing. The Great Ancestor was nothing and it was everything. The yearly offerings of syrup and wine that we poured into the Pit were still falling, because there was no end; maybe one year's wine had caught up to the previous year's, but none of it would stop until all prophecies had been fulfilled and the wine was absorbed into the Personage and the Personage knew how faithful the village had been and how to weave the Unending Darkness into our souls and lead us out beyond the stars. Clara Reed would have been plummeting now for just over a year, sticky from the syrup.

It was why I had been so afraid to jump. I had stayed awake into the night, imagining the sensation of falling blindly down until I lost consciousness or died and became part of the Ancestor. What would dying feel like if you couldn't see yourself? If you could only taste the air? Perhaps I wouldn't know that I had died, and would simply slip into death just as we slip between dreams. It still scared me: I was ashamed that a woman had jumped in my place. The act had not been performed correctly and I had been made false. If only I'd done what my dream had shown me, then the Anabatic Wind would have come by now, smoothing down the crops, rushing through the village like the breath from the very throat of the Ancestor itself. But I had stopped it from happening and I had broken the system of things. Like the snakes who had desired light, I had been selfish, and had thought only of myself.

I stood watching the boy, cleaning my hands with a cotton towel. The air was crisp and I could smell what each house on our side of the square had been cooking. Fish: swordtail, eel, red mullet. It was the first day of the New Year, and a time to celebrate. But the boy looked forlorn in his posture against the fountain. He reminded me of the pictures of the heroes from the old legends mother kept in her bedside table. Aorlius, whose lover was transformed by the Ancestor into a sprig of lavender, and Draxyx the traveller, who journeyed to the furthest constellations and in dying shaped the first light of the Bright Scar. The wax doll must mean a great deal to the boy. But why would he hang around the village square, making up stories about the Abyss? Perhaps something else was wrong, something he wasn't saying. If I were to go along with him, then I might be able to help.

I threw the towel onto the porch chair and marched down the steps. I had time: I was free now until 2 o' clock when we had class again, but Tsa Jin never took attendance. She'd never even learnt our names, she was too old. After that was Mass, but I could not miss that. The archivist and the diviner were to recite the Prophecy and give the year its name.

"What are you called?" I asked when I had reached the fountain.

"Sammy," he said.

"My name's Elin," I said.

Sammy said nothing. Just looked at me.

"Do you know exactly where they threw it?" I asked.

"Down in they Pit," the boy said. "It'm be by they Wailing Tree. They way down they stairs."

"Is that far from the village?" I asked. I'd never heard of a Wailing Tree.

"Out passing they Den," he said. "Off they track to they grain store."

"Not far from the flats," I said.

He shrugged.

"Let's see if we can't get your doll back," I said.

"Truthf'ly?" Sammy jumped to his feet, eyes widening. "Now we'll get it for shorn! I'n frighted to go by myself. It's too dark in this place."

"It's not dark in the day when the stars are out," I said.

"It is hawful dark," he said.

"Well, we can't be gone for too long," I said, beginning to walk towards the north street which led out of the square. Sammy caught up with me and we took the path which led to the outskirts of the village to the east.

Other girls passed us whom I knew from class and I tried desperately not to catch their eyes in case they told about me to Tsa Jin. They would talk among themselves, too, and make up silly things. I fingered a piece of candle in the pouch of my apron.

We came to the Den, a series of low, wooden sheds where the sour vapours of fermenting redberries caused my eyes and mouth to water. Outside, a row of barrels waited to be rolled into market. Some of them would go to the chapel and be consecrated in ritual. Then off to the Pit, just like us. Though the stars were out and pulsating in their usual rhythms, the land beyond the Den was dark. There were no street lamps this far out, just the faint seam of the Bright Scar. It appeared for a few hours during the middle of every day. It was a silver line across the sky which glimmered like an opal. Some said it was the Mouth of the Universe and therefore unholy because it represented the inverse of the Ancestor's emptiness. But I knew it was as the High Priest said: without the stars we would not know the grace of the Ancestor. We would not comprehend the darkness.

"Almost to it," said Sammy. We had walked for half a mile or so, bending gradually west towards the Pit. The boy kept close to my side and I was glad that he felt safe with me. I was glad also that he had some idea of where we were going, because I did not know this end of the village well. I was most familiar with the land to the east, where the banks of the Axis widened and the bracken grew thickest.

"One day I be gone up to where they's more than they stars," Sammy whispered as he stepped off the remnants of the dirt track. He hooked his fingers into my palm. "Daddun says."

"More than stars?" I said. "What do you mean?"

"Outer they sky."

"There is only the village," I insisted. "The village and the Abyss and the Personage."

"That's what your biggun's say, they priesties."

"Well it's the truth," I said. "It's the way of the life and the world."

"Life," said Sammy. The earth under my feet was full of grit and flint. It sang and cut at my shoe leather. "They's not nothing. Daddun says life be a cand-all in they dark."

"A candle flame is only given life in relation to the darkness," I said, remembering what I'd learnt in class. I removed the stick of wax from my apron and rolled it between my fingers.

"No'm," came Sammy's voice. He said nothing after that. Not until we had reached what I knew was the very lip of the Abyss. Its chill breath rose from the deep and rolled over us and I heard the echoes of the first prophecies. That's what Mother said it was, that hush of air, it was the First Word recreating itself, coming back again and again to speak into the silence.

Sammy bent to scan the ground, fingers pressed against his knees.

"What are you trying to find?" I asked.

"Shush," he said. "They Wailing."

I fell quiet, frowning. What could he mean, the wailing? Was it the tree he had been talking about? But then a new sound seemed to drift up from the Pit, a piping that reminded me of the wooden flute Grandmother had once owned. Mother now kept it in the bottom drawer of her sewing desk and would play it to me sometimes as I sat reading. It calmed me. Sammy spun around and stepped towards the edge. He took long, searching strides.

"Found it!" he said.

I followed his voice, straining my eyes, and discovered the boy bent over a small object. It was a piece of rock full of holes the size of my thumbnail. They might have been tunnels drilled by insects hundreds of years ago. The wind rose and flew through the holes like a musical instrument, making the same piping that

I'd thought came from the Pit. This, then, was the Wailing Tree. "They holy tree," said Sammy.

"It's like it's calling us," I said. "But where?"

"To they Pit," said Sammy. He rose and walked into the wind. A cloud must have passed over the stars, because for an instant I lost sight of him. Blinking hard, pushing colours into my head, I felt the stone at my feet.

"Sammy!" I called.

"Here!"

His voice came from below. I stood on the edge of the Abyss and made out his silver neck, his eyes reflecting the stars, as Sammy looked up at me in triumph.

"They steps," he said.

"There can't be *steps*," I said, feeling around the edge with my shoe. "Sammy?"

The Abyss yawned. Lightless, empty, unending. How could there be steps? How could anyone have thought to climb *down* into this place? It was forbidden.

"We shouldn't be here, Sammy," I said. My heart shook my voice.

"I'n know they way."

Sammy's own voice was receding, growing fainter. I lost sight of his head. *Sammy!* I wanted to scream. *Wait, for all the holy days of life, wait!* But I couldn't leave him by himself. Not out here.

Kneeling, I managed to descend to the ledge and follow Sammy down a shallow path which hugged the wall. The piping lessened to a whisper, and presently the starry sky became only a faint, narrow band over our heads.

"Sammy!" I shouted. "Please let's get back!"

"They doll's not far," came his voice. It sounded boxed up, encased in cloth or cotton.

I pressed my hand to the wall as I went. The rock wasn't dry as I'd expected, but was covered by a thin sleeve of moisture, like fruit that has just been washed. I concentrated on moving, on putting one foot in front of the other, for although the darkness wasn't an obstacle, the thought of the empty space caused my heart to patter even faster. The space that was the Personage. But I did not dwell on that for too long. If I caught up with Sammy, we could climb back to the surface. I would even make him a new doll if he liked.

I kept going for what must have been half an hour. My feet were beginning to ache and the air was growing colder, burning my throat so that I breathed only through my nose and as gently as possible. I scolded myself for not thinking to bring a cloak or a coat. I paused for rest, leaning against the wall of the Pit, and once my breathing had calmed, I realised that Sammy was further ahead than I'd first thought. The quiet was so complete that it squeezed against my inner ears. I screwed up my face and felt the sting of the cold on my eyes. This was true darkness. Darker even than the well in our yard, darker than night in my bedroom when I burrowed into the blankets. I had lost the stars.

"Sammy," I said. The word hissed like water on a hot grate.

I said it again a little louder. There was no echo this far down. The air felt so thin and so cold that it could no longer carry my voice. Perhaps the Personage did not allow for sound?

I tried once more, this time shouting Sammy's name as loud and for as long as I dared. The word felt raw around the edges and trembled on my lips. Colours returned, red velvet and lavender, dancing at the corners. And there, *there* — the tail end of an echo which sank away so quickly I almost missed it.

"They star."

Sammy's voice. It was quiet but clear, and came from somewhere below me. Not so far. I sighed and tucked my hands under my armpits, listening for it again.

"He'n winking at us."

Sammy was barely raising his voice: he couldn't be far. I placed a hand back on the wall, feeling the wet rock that suddenly put me in mind of the minnows from the river mum sometimes fried on Holy days.

"Stay where you are!" I called. "Don't go any further without me."

After another ten minutes of creeping and stumbling, my foot found a further ledge. Shifting blindly forward, waiting for the corner, I began to realise that there might not be another step. This might be the very bottom of the Abyss. Every breath shot to my head so that I felt as though I would fall. Did they know up there? Did any of the priests, the archivists and their recording, did they know that the Abyss had an end? The ground sloped a little. Eventually it evened out and I paused, breathing quietly.

"Didn' I say right?" Sammy's voice escaped from the air in front.

"Is this really it?" I asked. "This is as far as it goes?"

"Listen to they river," he said.

We both fell silent. There, like a picture that suddenly slips in from the back of your mind, the soft rush of water. It couldn't be far from us, perhaps only a few feet. I took another step, holding a hand out in case I walked into Sammy. This kind of darkness was still new to me. Another four steps and the trickling was directly in front of me. A skin of ice. My hand broke it open, all the way to the wrist. It was shallow, a ribbon of water moving across the sloping rock, following the wall of the Abyss. Where had it come from? The Axis curved in from the flats; we drank from it before it carried on into the dark, but it did not approach the Abyss, as far as I knew.

"What should we do?" I asked. *Go back,* I almost answered myself. *Go home.*

"See they flickeryin' star. They's where my doll is."

I had missed it entirely: a pinprick of light a star, as bright as any in the sky, but here it was on its own and low to the ground, pressed in by the Abyss. It looked as though we could approach it, even walk towards it. I stared at the tiny, quivering thing and the air seemed to move. Colours flared at the edges, glowing and pulsing. The blood pounded through my head and I did not even think to feel the cold.

"How do you know it's there?" I asked, the words almost catching in my throat. Like a daddy longlegs latching itself to a windowpane.

"I been there," said Sammy. "There's a way outer they Pit."

"A way out?"

"By they star."

Looking over my shoulder, I saw the star imprinted onto the darkness and as my eyes moved back, it followed in broken lines, scoring itself into my vision.

"The river's flowing in the same direction," I said. "We can follow the water."

"Warty star," Sammy chuckled. *Water star.*

There was a stream, I remembered as we shuffled alongside the flow, in the stories about Draxyx and the Ancestor. It had cooled his feet on his journey from star to star. The Ancestor had appeared as a shadow on the water.

In some places, the rock bed was as slimy as the walls and it became impossible to scramble further without use of our hands. Spider-like, we became creatures with long, wet limbs. We took sips from the water and it numbed our throats. Sharp gullies caused the river to spray and we had to feel for the connecting rock. My soft shoes were almost useless.

"It's bigger," I said. "The star. Twice the size, can you see?"

But Sammy did not seem to be listening. He was clambering over the rocks ahead, silhouette breaking through the starlight. There were scrapes and flat splashes as he slipped, grunting to himself, murmuring questions.

I found him crouched by a lip of rock, the edge of a small aperture in the ground. Every now and again, a wave of loose water was shunted into the hole, where it resounded with a slap. Sammy was gripping the rim, peering into the dark.

"Can you see anything down there?" I said.

"Need they light, Elly," he breathed.

"The light?" I asked.

"They cand-all," he said. "They waxy."

"Oh," I said. I drew out the heel of white candle. The taper was dry, but I had no way to light it. Wait. I felt the breast pocket of my cardigan, and yes — a pair of matches, wrapped in a fold of striking paper.

Shadows rippled on the rock as I lowered the flame, holding it out of reach of the water. There was something down there. I caught the gleam of a small white figure in the dark.

"They's mine," said Sammy.

"That's your doll?" I asked. I drew back the candle to steady myself. I looked to the star. It was edged with blue and no longer twinkled in the same way.

"They light, Elly," Sammy said again, nudging my arm.

Hot wax fell as I brought the flame back. The doll was there alright, just beneath the surface of the water. It stared up at us, expressionless.

I was about to speak, to suggest that one of us try to fish it out, when Sammy stirred. A voice was coming from the star, muttering and echoing. Too indistinct to make out what it was saying. With a scrape of his feet, Sammy leapt across the opening.

"Sammy, wait!"

Still warm, the wax shaped itself to my fist as I ran. I slipped and banged my knees, but lumbered on. The light had doubled in size. The river sparkled and divided into pools. By the glint of polished rock above, I realised that the Abyss had narrowed and had twisted into a tunnel. *The light*, I remembered. *She will come to the light of the stars and be reborn.* What if this was all part of the prophecy? What if the Ancestor were waiting at the end to wrap me in dark arms and send me back to the village? The star filled the way, its rays piercing the walls. I was blind. The light stung: even with my lids squeezed shut it still burned a way through.

The Abyss came to an end. I walked out of it, both hands shielding my eyes from the burning starlight. A cold wind swept my hair back and something rustled like sweetgrass in the fields. Was this how a star was meant to feel? The wind came again, stronger this time. I'd never felt it so strong. It fell to a low breeze and brought with it the scent of sweet grass when it is added to hot water and the steam billows around the room. Less familiar scents, too, though pleasant. Taking a sharp breath, I raised my hands and made myself look out.

Fields like the patchwork quilt my mother worked on in the evenings. The strange, warm pink of a sky, deep and unending. I was on the side of a great hill. The cold waters trickled out through crevices in the rocks to join a wider river that snaked towards — what was that? A precise line where the sky met the fields. And above it, a circle of orange light as big as a copper plate. It hurt to look at its face. My head pounded and hummed, pushing tears down the sides of my nose. Where was this? It was all so *bright*. So distant. Had Sammy meant for me to come here?

I strode forward from the opening onto a plateau of long grass, hands shielding my eyes, and turned to inspect the hill. Its slopes climbed for what must have been a mile, I couldn't tell. A further, smaller peak emerged from its rear as if it desired one day to break away. The sun was laughing at me. I heard its chatter. Where was our sky? The darkness and the stars?

"Down there!"

A shout to my left. There were people on the hillside just above me, four of them, descending on a thin track which wound its way up and disappeared into vegetation.

"You down there!" came the call again.

Their cheeks were red and they wore bright clothing, one man leading, two women behind him. They each carried a basket on their arm. I could not see what else to do, so I waited. But I would be ready to run, if there was a way.

"Are you lost?" the man said. He placed a foot on a stone made wet by the river. "You're both lucky we were foraging this side of they mountain. Not many come out this far."

A shout came from behind the women.

"Elly!"

It was Sammy. I said nothing, but studied the man's face. It was wrinkled and dark, although he might have been younger than mother.

"Miss Elly helpin' me find they way again," said Sammy, coming forward to place a hand on the man's forearm. He seemed to have taken on a new way of moving in this bright place, confident and tall. Older, I might have guessed.

"Fact is," the man said, his voice lowered as if confiding in me a terrible secret. "Sammy here went missing on this trail not long afore now. His daddy will be greatly pleased."

"Where am I?" I asked.

"Red Mountains," the man frowned. "I don't see you in they camp afore."

"Stephen," the older woman said, taking a step towards me. "See how pale she is. She'n not from they camp. She'n one of them from they *inside*."

"From yon Pit, Stevie," Sammy nodded.

"Now you say it," the man peered closer at me. "You could be right."

"See her eyes, too," said the woman. "Bigger'n ours."

"Is that a sun?" I asked, looking behind me to the circle of orange light.

"Don't insiders know they sun?" he said.

"Course not," said the woman. "I hear they seein' they holes in they Red Mountains and call them stars."

"Well, if you'n say so," said the man.

He offered his hand. Its palm was creased with dirt, fingers thick and blistered.

"Better you be coming with us."

I took a step back. "The Personage sent you?"

"They purse on?" he grinned.

"Be they god," said the older woman. "You don't know they stories? They left to worship they new god. A crazy, willifying god whom bides in they dark. They say they priesties made up they future in a list and now they follow them year on year."

"No god like that here, girly," said the man, his hand still outstretched. 'No stories, neither."

Glancing over my shoulder, I saw the sun behind, glowing gold near the break of the sky like a pool of molten iron. *She will come to the light of the stars and be reborn.* This man did not know the Personage. There was no going with him, or any of them. I would not stay here on this hill. I would go to the sun: by the time I reached it, it might have settled in the fields.

Springing away from the foragers, and with a last look at Sammy, I leapt into the thicket where the river vanished and began to pick a path down the mountain. I ignored their yells, shrugged them off like whining flies. I would follow the course of the river, like Draxyx from star to star, with the Ancestor as my companion. I would come to the sun, bring it back for the village.

I darted between low-growing trees, listening for water, pausing in the undergrowth to breathe in the new smells. I felt a warm glow on the backs of my hands, my arms, my cheeks. What year would it be now? What would the Personage have named it? The Year that Elin Reached the Sun. The Year of the Bright Lands.

See Felix Taylor's story "The Year of the Bright Lands" online at Metaphorosis.
If you liked it, leave a comment. Authors love that!
Remember to subscribe to our e-mail updates so you'll know when new stories are posted.

About the story

The idea to write 'The Year of the Bright Lands' came with an image of a row of crops suspended over an abyss, buffeted around by a mysterious wind from below. Then came the decision to write a story about two children who find a way down into the abyss. I don't usually go for plot when I start writing, so I began with a voice and the image of the abyss and constructed the narrative around it. I quickly scrapped the suspended crops, but the abyss was interesting. What if people lived nearby and worshipped it as their conception of eternity? As the story took shape, I realised that there were certain threads I wanted to explore, such as the implications for a religion based on darkness, and how life might work without sunlight. As for where it went after that, I find that most stories I write end in *deus ex machina* or what Tolkien called 'eucatastrophe' — something mystical happens out of the blue with nothing to account for it. It's never satisfying for the editors who read them, and it's just an easy way out for me who doesn't have to think about a good conclusion. This was the case for the first draft of 'The Year of the Bright Lands', and the editor, justifiably, didn't take to it. Which made me stop and think, and the story ended up a far better creation because of it.

A question for the author

Q: If you could have a meal with a character from any classic novel, whom would you choose?

A: I think a picnic on the river with Rat from *Wind in the Willows* would be something special, if only for the landscape. Otherwise it might be Dostoyevsky's idiot, Prince Myshkin, for his beautiful nature and frank conversation.

About the author

Felix Taylor is a writer and librarian, living in Oxford, UK. His work tends towards the weird and fantastic. As an ex-academic, he has published on Arthur Machen, John Cowper Powys, and animal ethics.

Copyright

Title information

Metaphorosis March 2022

ISSN: 2573-136X (online)
ISBN: 978-1-64076-224-4 (e-book)
ISBN: 978-1-64076-225-1 (paperback)

Copyright

Publisher

Metaphorosis Magazine is an imprint of
Metaphorosis Publishing
Neskowin, OR, USA

www.metaphorosis.com

"Metaphorosis" is a registered trademark.

Discounts available

Substantial discounts are available for educational institutions, including writing workshops. Discounts are also available for quantity purchases. For details, contact Metaphorosis at metaphorosis.com/about

Metaphorosis Publishing

Metaphorosis offers beautifully written science fiction and fantasy. Our imprints include:

Metaphorosis Magazine
Plant Based Press
Verdage
Vestige

You can also find us:
@MetaphorosisMag, @MetaphorosisRev, @Metaphorosis
www.facebook.com/metaphorosis

Help keep Metaphorosis running by supporting us at
Patreon.com/metaphorosis

See more about some of our books on the following pages.

Metaphorosis Magazine

Metaphorosis

a magazine of speculative fiction

Metaphorosis is an online speculative fiction magazine dedicated to quality writing. We publish an original story every week, along with author bios, interviews, and notes on story origins.

We also publish monthly print and e-book issues, as well as yearly Best of and Complete anthologies.

Come and see us online at magazine.Metaphorosis.com.

Plant Based Press

Vegan-friendly science fiction and fantasy, including anthologies of the year's best SFF stories, from 2016-2020.

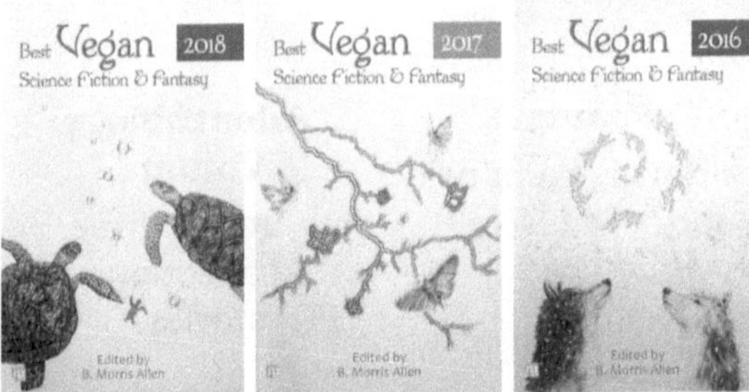

Chambers of the Heart

*speculative stories
by
B. Morris Allen*

A heart that's a building, a dog that's a program, a woman sinking irretrievably — stories about love, loss, and movement.

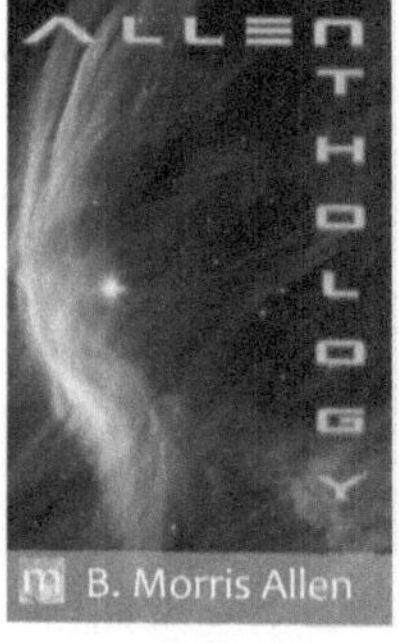

Susurrus

A darkly romantic story of magic, love, and suffering.

Allenthology: Volume I

Including three full collections of SFF stories.

Verdage

Science fiction and fantasy books for writers – full of great stories, often with an additional focus on the craft of speculative fiction writing.

Reading 5X5 x2

Duets

How do authors' voices change when they collaborate?

A round-robin of five talented science fiction and fantasy authors collaborating with each other and writing solo.

Including stories by Evan Marcroft, David Gallay, J. Tynan Burke, L'Erin Ogle, and Douglas Anstruther.

Score

an SFF symphony

An anthology with
an emotional score
from the heights of
joy to the depths of
despair – but always
with a little hope
shining through.

Reading 5X5

*Five stories, five
times*

See how different
writers take on
the same material.

Reading 5X5

Writers' Edition

Two extra stories,
the story seed,
and authors' notes
on writing.

Vestige

Novelettes, novellas, and novels by Metaphorosis authors.

The Nocturnals
Mariah Montoya

Night is Dangerous.
Day is deadly.

Where day and night last thirty years, humans move constantly stay ahead of the night and cruel Nocturnals that call it home. But a boy is lost out there.